Death in a Hot Flash

A Bel Barrett Mystery

JANE ISENBERG

This is a work of fiction. Names, characters, places, and incidents either are the product of the author's imagination or are used fictitiously. Any resemblance to actual events, locales, organizations, or persons, living or dead, is entirely coincidental and beyond the intent of either the author or the publisher.

AVON BOOKS, INC.
An Imprint of HarperCollins*Publishers*
10 East 53rd Street
New York, New York 10022-5299

Inside cover author photo by Stephanie Violette
Published by arrangement with the author
Library of Congress Catalog Card Number: 99-94988
ISBN: 0-380-80281-3
www.harpercollins.com

First Avon Books Printing: February 2000

Printed in the U.S.A.

WCD 10 9 8 7 6 5 4 3 2 1

To Bel Kaufman,
whose *Up the Down Staircase*
has inspired me for decades

Acknowledgments

Some writers sequester themselves with their PCs or legal pads and write in contemplative solitude. I am not one of them. When I am at work on a book, I reach out to others for all sorts of help, so I want to acknowledge those who provided it this time around. For sharing generously their wisdom and expertise, I am grateful to Rick Comes; Elaine Foster; Dr. Annette Hollander; the staff at the Jersey Room of the Jersey City Public Library; Gary Kwiatkowski; Judy and Burt Lavine; Ross London; Frank Mlynarczyk; Joan Rafter; Jimmy Shamburg, Deputy Police Director, Jersey City, New Jersey; Denise Swanson Stybr; Ruth Tait; and Susan Tompkins. For bringing the series to the attention of my editor, Jennifer Sawyer Fisher, I thank my supportive agent, Laura Blake Peterson. I really appreciate Jennifer's sleuth-savvy sensibility. My writing group members—Susan Babinski; Pat Juell; and Rebecca Mlynarczyk have once again won the prize for tact, patience, and inspired manuscript critiquing. For managing somehow "to be there for me" as my students would say, without actually being here at all, I send love to Rachel and Daniel Isenberg and Brian Stoner. And for managing "to be there for me" while really being here, no mean feat either, I embrace my husband, Phil Tompkins.

Chapter 1

January 10, 1996

Dear Ma Bel,

Are you serious about teaching writing to a bunch of undertakers? Just think: my mom, morticians' muse.

Trust me Mom, Israel is nothing like you fantasize. Nobody here is sitting around thinking about terrorists. There hasn't even been a bombing since November. So stop stressing out over everything you read in the papers. You're in more danger in downtown Jersey City than I am at Shemayim. That's the name of my kibbutz. I think it's Hebrew for heaven. *It's awesome. The Mediterranean is a two-minute walk from our dorm.*

And my work assignment isn't going to be in the concrete slab factory after all. No, your son is going to be picking up trash on the beach and doing some landscaping. (Yes, I'll wear the damn sunblock you stuck in my duffel bag.) So far, being a kibbutznik beats the hell out of temping on Wall Street. My most stressful chore here will be finding someone to rub the sunblock on my back. (There are only eight women in our group of forty.)

I hope spring semester goes okay. Don't let those embalmers get under your skin. Sorry, bad joke.

Love,
Mark

I knew my son would have something to say when I wrote him about my spring schedule. So did children's lit professor Wendy O'Connor, friend and office mate. "What the hell are you doing teaching in the Funeral Service Ed Program? That's pretty kinky even for you, Bel." As she spoke, Wendy was frantically ferreting through files, looking for her bibliography on Beatrix Potter, which she needed to take with her on sabbatical to England. In the flurry of her search, she had scattered folders, papers, and books all over her desk and the floor. I struggled to stifle my inner neatnik's knee-jerk reaction to the evidence that Wendy's whirlwind quest had made a shambles of our tiny office in the River Edge Community College English Department.

"Wanna trade places? I'll fly to the Lake District on sabbatical tomorrow and do research on Beatrix and you can stay here in Jersey City and teach the undertaker wanna-bes. This is my last offer. Take it or leave it," I said, not even looking up from the syllabus I was revising for the upcoming semester. If I raised my head, Wendy might notice the unbecoming shade of green that envy had tinted my complexion. Besides, I didn't want to have to look at the mess she had made.

"No thanks. But I really do want to know how you ended up teaching in the FSE Program. You may be a hormonally challenged postmenopausal flake, Bel, but let me remind you that you once majored in English lit at Vassar. And you wrote a damn good master's thesis on models for matriarchy in Virginia Woolf. So how on earth did you wind up as a matriarch yourself, teaching future undertakers and embalmers? Did the dean ask you to do it? Suddenly, Wendy waved a folder under my nose. "Eureka!" Her elfin face was lit by a triumphant grin.

"No, it wasn't the dean this time." Even *I* could hear the whine of resignation in my voice. "It was Vinny Vallone. I let that silver-tongued Svengali wheedle me into co-teaching with him."

"Okay. Now *that* I can almost understand," said Wendy, bending to gather folders from the floor. "I've heard he really is a spinmeister. Exactly how did he convince you? Come on, Bel, this is your last chance to tell Wendy."

She was right. One of the qualities I most appreciate about Wendy is her affinity for gossip. I was especially going to miss our Sunday-morning walks at Liberty State Park where, in the name of fitness, we would spend an hour swapping stories about our colleagues and trashing the ever entertaining RECC administration. "Okay. Okay. Let's see, first he practically purred into my ear about how much fun it would be for us to co-teach. An 'utter hoot' was how he put it." And when that didn't get to me, he tried flattery."

"Oh no. That would *never* work with you," cracked Wendy. Her deadpan voice belied the smile that had nudged up the corners of her mouth.

"Well, it was a long shot, but he was desperate," I fired back. "Anyway, you know how Vinny loves really bad jokes and puns. So he said that just the other day somebody had told him I was such a gifted teacher that I could inspire even a corpse to write well." I smirked.

Wendy put down the armful of books she had picked up from the floor and held her nose.

Ignoring her gesture, I went on. "I must have looked aghast, because then Vinny really cranked up the wheedle and tried to bribe me."

Wendy was giggling now. "Let me guess. He offered you food, right?"

"Damn, Wendy, you know me too well. But of course you're right. That incorrigible man actually promised he'd whip up gourmet lunches for me during all our planning sessions. At his palazzo in Paulus Hook, no less. Where would he ever get the idea that I can be bought for the price of a good feed?"

"So you sold yourself for a meal and a house tour, Bel? Is that what you're telling me?" Wendy prodded. I was surprised when she added, "Actually, I'd love to see that house. Paulus Hook's such a great old neighborhood too, full of those to-die-for historic homes. I have a friend living there who says Vinny really put a fortune into his renovation."

"He's very pumped about it, that's for sure. But no, I didn't 'sell myself for a meal and a house tour,' " I replied rather primly. "I hate to disappoint you, but I have my professional principles, my scholarly integrity. And that's exactly what he appealed to next."

"I give up. Tell me what he said already." Wendy had stood up and was stuffing several books and the bibliography into her knapsack.

"Oh, he just went on about how important it was for the FSE students to know how to write well and do research," I recounted.

"So is that what finally got you to agree to work

with him?" Wendy had begun to re-shelve the books remaining on her desk.

"No. That wasn't what did it either. Actually, I was trying to formulate a refusal that would leave his ego intact and me with at least a vestige of academic credibility. But check this out. You'll love it. Before I could say a word, the man actually got down on one knee and went into this long riff on how the funeral service industry is finally beginning to attract women, but how there's not a single woman teaching in the program here at RECC." I had to smile as I recalled the sight of my portly colleague struggling up from the floor.

Wendy must have had the same image, because she chortled and said, "Well, he knew just what buttons of yours to push." Now she was filing folders she had pulled out earlier.

"He sure did. He said our female students need at least one 'absolutely fabulous feminist female professor.' "

"Jesus," said Wendy, rolling her eyes.

"A few more sessions like that and Vinny had me convinced that I was born to undertake the education of undertakers, that there was little I would rather do, and furthermore, that the future of feminism in the funeral industry depended on my doing so."

Sighing, Wendy said, "You're easy, Bel. That's your whole problem."

"Easy maybe, but stupid, no. You better believe I didn't capitulate without negotiating." When I responded to her charge, there was a defensive edge to my voice. Wendy always got on me for being a soft touch when a colleague needed a favor. "I said I'd co-teach Funeral Service History: Writing and Research only if Vinny would keep a teaching journal and let me analyze it as part of a project for the graduate course I'm taking in classroom research. And he agreed to that."

"Well Bel, at least you're not the only one susceptible to the charms of Vinny Vallone," Wendy said. "I heard that he held a clandestine meeting at the funeral parlor he and his brother own—"

"Vallone and Sons," I interjected.

"Whatever," said Wendy, eager now to share her news. "At this secret meeting in the chamber of death, he somehow persuaded all of RECC's adjuncts to unionize. Isn't that impressive?"

"Yes, especially since President Woodman is totally opposed to the unionization of part-timers." My voice sounded weary. RECC's over-reliance on a ragtag band of exploited adjunct faculty members was same old same old. Likewise, Woodman's anti-union stance was yesterday's news.

"I just don't see how people can live on what they pay adjuncts." With that, Wendy wedged the last book into the bookcase.

"I know. It's Dickensian. Part-timers get a mere pittance for what amounts to academic piecework. No health benefits or anything. But listen, if they unionize . . ." I paused, imagining the possibilities inherent in the new scenario.

"That's what Vinny figured. And he's in a good position to speak out. After all, he's got a real day gig as partner in Vallone and Sons. It was pretty decent of him, actually." Wendy sounded thoughtful as she carefully dusted her newly cleared desktop.

"He's a decent guy. Just a little over-the-top sometimes, that's all." I had given up getting anything more done on my syllabus and began packing my book bag. I added, "He's the one who actually persuaded RECC to start the Funeral Service Ed Program because he wanted to see more inner-city young people get into the funeral business. According to him, it's not only lucrative, but it's also fulfilling. I mean he can be a pain in the ass, but he does some good things."

"I'll drink to that. Unless you're reneging on your promise to treat me to a farewell lunch at Laico's." Wendy was standing at the door surveying our suddenly tidy cubicle. As I locked up, she pointed at the two veteran philodendrons, spindly green survivors that had graced our windowsill for over five years, and said, "Don't forget to water Thelma and Louise. And you'd better write me all about what it's like teaching the undertakers of tomorrow."

Once the semester began, teaching the "undertakers of tomorrow," did in fact, turn out to be the "utter hoot" Vinny had promised, at least sometimes. I would most certainly have a lot to write Wendy about. In spite of all the reservations I'd had about co-teaching in the FSE Program, working with Vinny was often very inspiring. That man could get students really worked up over long-ago pharaonic funerals. He described those ancient rituals so vividly one could swear there was a freshly swathed mummy laid out atop the next desk. But then sometimes when the nuances of classroom management eluded him, Vinny turned to me for mentoring.

There was one particular day when he was really upset. We were having lunch at the RIP, a nearby diner where, for lack of any cafeteria facilities of our own, RECC faculty and students often eat. Vinny sudddenly confided, "Bel, I'm absolutely flummoxed. What's a poor adjunct to do?" And he looked flummoxed too, kind of rumpled and wrinkled instead of his usual smooth and unruffled self. He leaned across the table and lowered his voice. "I wouldn't tell anyone except you about this, but one of our students, a woman, has been sort of following me around." I knew Vinny had never married and I thought he lived alone, so I wasn't too surprised to note that he made being followed by a woman sound about as appealing as waking up with cat barf on the pillow. When I looked skeptical, he hurried to explain: "Yes. She is, Bel. She's really following me. There's no other way to describe it. She leaves me notes too."

"Who is it?" I asked, trying to imagine which one of our three female students might be capable of such behavior.

"It's Eleanor Chambers, Bel. Can you imagine? I'm absolutely deranged." And Vinny grabbed his shirt front and began tugging on it in a very convincing display of derangement.

"Vinny, your soup is getting cold. Leave your shirt alone and have your soup." I didn't usually mother Vinny, but somehow mothering seemed an appropriate response just then while I was trying to recall Eleanor Chambers. I'd only seen her once or twice because she had missed a lot of classes. She hadn't handed in much work either. I remembered her as a tall and rangy white woman in her thirties with brownish hair.

"Now why on earth would Eleanor follow you around? What does she say in these notes? You know, Eleanor hasn't been in class lately. And why haven't you said anything to me about this before? You haven't mentioned it in your teaching journal." I was still in mother mode.

Without touching his soup, Vinny explained, "Oh

I mentioned it this week, all right. Here," he handed me a folder of yellow papers, each covered with his inimitable and nearly illegible scrawl. Vinny had not yet invested in a laptop, and he preferred to write his teaching journals at home rather than word process them at the busy funeral parlor. So he always scribbled in longhand on legal pads, and I always complained about his handwriting. This exchange had become a ritual. But before I could voice my usual line about decoding Sanskrit, he was talking again. "I saw Eleanor in the parking lot last Tuesday right after she had left a note under my windshield wiper. She absolutely gives me the creeps, Bel."

"Why? She seems harmless to me. What was her note about? Did she say why she's been missing class?" I pushed away my empty soup cup and waited for our waitress to bring my tuna sandwich.

"Bel, her note says she knows how I feel about her and she hopes we can get together soon. She thinks I won't say anything in class about how much I care for her because of the other students." As Vinny spoke he lowered his voice, and I had to lean across the table to catch his last words.

"Oh, Vinny. You mean she has a crush on you! It's a nuisance, I know, but she'll get over it." Vinny was handsome in a boyish, fortyish sort of way, and quite charming when he chose to be. He was going to have to get used to handling students with crushes. We all did. It goes with the territory, especially if you're young and attractive. "Eleanor does seem a bit old for that sort of thing, though. I mean she's in her thirties, isn't she?" My tone was still light. I couldn't understand why Vinny didn't seem to be responding with his own usual lightness.

"Bel, this is serious. This woman calls me and

leaves utterly outrageous messages. Yesterday she left one with my secretary at the funeral parlor. And now she's started calling me at home too. I absolutely dread retrieving my messages. What am I going to do? She's driving me crazy, Bel."

"It does sound as if Eleanor's harassing you. Why not discuss it with the FSE counselor? Perhaps she can call Eleanor in for a chat." My tone was no longer light. The woman did sound a bit out of bounds. Poor Vinny. He didn't have much teaching experience, and most of the women he regularly interacted with were either widows shopping for coffins or those already in what he delicately called an "altered state." No wonder he was overreacting.

"If I report her, Bel, she might deny it or, worse yet, Batty Hattie might accuse *me* of harassing Eleanor." He was right. I'd forgotten about Hattie Majors, sister-in-law to a Jersey City commissioner and hired at his request as a counselor at RECC. It was actually Vinny who had dubbed her "Batty Hattie" after she registered all thirty-five FSE students for Embalming III before they had taken Orientation to Embalming. The name had stuck. Ever since, Hattie had been bad-mouthing Vinny to anyone who would listen. "You know how that goes now. Eleanor might sue. And besides, she's not my only problem." Now Vinny looked around the RIP, his dark eyes darting here and there as if he were expecting Eleanor to materialize in a neighboring booth.

"Are you being followed by other women?" Without meaning to, I let my tone get flip again. But the image of my pudgy colleague playing pied piper to a parade of panting females *was* amusing.

"No, Bel. This is different. But it's just as bad. It's Henry Granger."

Now I nodded knowingly, picturing Henry, another one of our shared students. Henry Granger was a muscular, dark-skinned African-American man in his early twenties with two teardrops tattooed beneath his left eye. My friend Illuminada Guttierez, who's a private investigator, had told me these were very likely gang markers indicating that he'd killed two people. In combination with his trademark black jcans and black sweatshirt, his tattoos gave Henry an aura of slightly grim glamour. But when I'd taught him last semester in Speech, he'd given a talk detailing his religious conversion in prison. Then he had impressed us all with his commitment to starting a business in the inner city and to working with the youth group at his church. "Don't tell me you think Henry's in love with you?" My tone here was a bit snide.

"Bel, you're going out of your way to be bitchy. Didn't you take your estrogen today?" Vinny was scoring high in the bitchy department himself, but I forgave him because I could see he was really upset. "Henry Granger is absolutely livid with me because I gave him an F on his outline and nixed his research topic."

"What's his topic again?" I asked, simultaneously cursing my unreliable memory and trying harder to respond to my colleague's obvious and growing distress.

"I'm not sure. That's the problem. But the title is, would you believe, 'Gangsta Grief.' I mean really, Bel, what the hell is that supposed to mean?" Vinny sounded genuinely puzzled.

"Right. Of course. I remember now. How could I forget that great title? Actually I meant to speak to you about Henry's topic. He's researching grieving rituals among those coping with gang-related killings.

He's interviewing family members, surviving gang members, clergy, funeral directors, and doing a lot of library research."

Now I was angry, so I kept talking. "And what's wrong with that topic, Vinny? The loss of young African-American males is a tragic part of modern American history. Right here in Jersey City they're dying in record numbers. Don't you think all the funerals of gunned-down fifteen-year-olds are worth studying? Don't you think we could learn something from looking at the grieving rituals of their communities? I thought that's what this course was all about." I sat back and waited for a response from Vinny, who was looking, as he would say, "absolutely" shell-shocked.

"Good grief, Bel, how the hell am I supposed to know about all that? I'm an undertaker, not a sociologist. I thought it was some sort of rap thing, like a joke. I didn't look at it at all the way you describe it. Of course, you're probably right. Oh God. Right under the F I wrote, 'This is not an appropriate topic for a college paper.' When I handed him the paper, he looked at it, gathered his books, stood up and stomped out of the room." Vinny was wide-eyed as he recalled Henry's exit. "I know you're fond of him, Bel, but I have to admit he scares me." Vinny glanced at me sheepishly and, putting his elbows on the table, supported his head between his hands.

"Oh for God's sake, Vinny. Don't be such a racist wimp. Talk to him," I urged, trying to keep exasperation from sharpening my voice. "Explain. Apologize. Then try to help him with the paper. Listen to him."

Vinny looked up, and when he spoke, resolve had brightened his voice, "Listen Bel, I may be a wimp, but I'm not racist. And you're right. Absolutely. I'll talk to him after class tommorrow."

Unfortunately, Vinny didn't show up for class the next day. When Dean Haskins asked me to cover Vinny's portion of our shared course, I agreed. When Vinny didn't return calls to his home or answer e-mail, I assumed he had succumbed to the flu of the month. I tried to reach him at the funeral parlor. He hadn't been there either, and he hadn't called in sick. The receptionist told me that Victor Vallone, Vinny's brother and partner, was worried. He had stopped by Vinny's house. Vinny wasn't there. Victor had reported him missing.

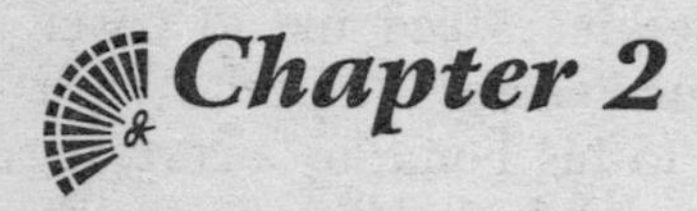

Chapter 2

To: Bbarrett@circle.com
From: Rbarrett@UWash.edu
Re: Man's world
Date: 01/12/96 10:16:48

Dear Mom,

I wish you'd stop stressing yourself out about Mark. He's a big boy now. And I really think he's safe on the beach. Think about it, Mom. Where would a suicide bomber masquerading as a beach bum hide the bomb? In his bikini briefs? NOT. Just try to get over it, all right? I don't want to worry about you worrying.

But if you really want to worry about something, did you ever stop to wonder why my brother's spending his days on a Mediterranean beach, my boyfriend's biking up and down various local mountains every weekend, your boyfriend (well, what *do* you want me to call Sol?) is doing God knows what in Eastern Europe, and you and I are working and studying all the time? Have I been genetically programmed to labor endlessly or do I have a choice?

Actually, things are going fairly well this quarter. They pretty much give me the hours I need at the restaurant now and classes are okay.

I hope you are not shoveling all that snow yourself. Mark and Sol sure knew when to bail, right? Pay somebody to do it, please.

Rebecca

Rebecca was probably right. Mark would be fine. But I couldn't help worrying about him anyway and my daily on-line doses of the *Jerusalem Post*'s reports on the latest mayhem in the Middle East did little to assuage my fears.

And I was worried about Vinny too. Where the hell was he? During the classes of his that I was covering, our students learned more than they ever wanted to know about writing up research and nothing about funerals through the ages. Adding that extra class to my schedule meant I was teaching eighteen credits a week instead of the usual fifteen.

Just when I thought I would collapse from exhaustion under a mountain of student writing, Vinny turned up.

Unfortunately he turned up in the Jersey City morgue. A carpenter doing renovation work at the marina's restaurant spotted Vinny's bloated corpse afloat in the Morris Canal. The police retrieved the body right away. Sadly, even though Vinny had been a familiar figure at the morgue, no one there recognized his waterlogged and rock-scraped remains. But thanks to Vinny's penchant for engraved gold jewelry, the police quickly ascertained his name and spotted it on the list of local missing persons.

It was a lot harder and took a lot longer for me to believe that Vinny was dead. Even the screaming headlines surrounding a color photo of him on the front page of the morning edition of the *Jersey City Herald* didn't make sense to me at first. When our class met later that day, I was still struggling to come to terms with Vinny's death.

A little-known fact that teachers soon discover is that a surefire way to learn something is to teach it to someone else. It fell to me to help Vinny's students understand and accept the loss of a man who, as their teacher and academic advisor, had been the only real mentor some of them had ever known. A few students had seen the morning paper and spread word of Vinny's death to the others, so that by the time I entered the room, the air was heavy with their shock and sadness. As if they sought to comfort themselves with logic, they were formulating explanations for how Vinny had ended up in the canal. Their explanations were all shocking to me.

"What he want to go and kill hisself for? He wasn't too old and he had a good business," asked Joevelyn Tate, a plump young woman who was clearly holding back tears. "He always acted so happy." Joevelyn often claimed that when Vinny had recruited her to the Funeral Services Education Program, he transformed her life. "Without him talkin' to me 'bout this program, I be cleanin' offices at night for the rest of my days," was how she put it.

Suicide? Vinny? I tried to imagine what might have driven Vinny to drown himself, but before I could conjure up any possibilities, Alan Weiner spoke up, "But Professor Vallone was Catholic. Catholics aren't supposed to commit suicide." Alan was always so literal, and he was young. He still believed that people did only what they were supposed to do. But I thought he was right. Vinny *was* Catholic, and I knew that, until his mother's death last year, he'd frequently accompanied her to church.

"I know, Alan, you're right. But Professor Vallone's mother died last year. Of cancer. She had been sick for a long time. Maybe he had a sort of delayed reaction to her illness and death. Maybe he had become depressed." I was really reaching, grasping for a way to explain an inexplicable act, thinking out loud, really.

"Professor Vallone told me all about his mother and how she passed on. That's why he suggested I do my research paper on the hospice movement. He sounded like he was pretty cool about his mother's passing. He didn't want her to suffer no more." This from Amado Ramos, living, I knew, with his own mother's struggle with breast cancer.

Just then Gilberto Hernandez arrived, nodding politely at me as if to apologize for his tardiness, but not actually saying anything. Gilberto had been doing an externship at Vallone and Sons, so I assumed that he had known Vinny better than the others. Because he wasn't usually late, I decided not to make an issue of it. There were clearly extenuating circumstances that day.

Gilberto had flashing dark eyes and an easy grin and was handsome in a male-model sort of way. But as he took his seat that day, his eyes were still and his lips were a straight slash across his face.

I resolved to do more listening than speaking, since I had no insight to offer and since the students clearly wanted to talk. "Please take one of these and pass the rest," I said, handing Alan a sheaf of announcements about Vinny's wake and funeral. The familiar classroom routine of passing around printed material occupied us for a moment or two.

Then, while she was stuffing the handout into her book bag, Joevelyn blurted out, "You know, maybe he got bad news or somethin', like, you know, his health . . ." Her words hung suspended in the room, catching all of us off guard. Of course, she could be right. How much did any of us know about Vinny, really? Vinny had never mentioned a word to me about being sick, but would he have? For all his chattiness, Vinny had always kept his private life private. It was awful to think of him hiding a serious health problem behind a facade of bad puns. Poor soul. Joevelyn must have been thinking the same thing, because her eyes were tearing up again.

"Maybe he was worried about somethin', like, you know, maybe somebody had somethin' on him." It was Henry Granger, speculating so matter-of-factly in his deep voice that Joevelyn stopped blowing her nose and, along with the rest of us, turned toward Henry, a dark face in our circle.

As usual, Alan required more information. "You mean you think somebody might have been threatening to blackmail Professor Vallone?" Alan's voice approached a squeak when he got to Vinny's name. "So instead of calling the cops or paying the blackmailer, he jumped in the river? Is that what you *really* think?" Alan looked incredulous. In his own carefully ordered version of the universe, such a series of events was out of the question.

"Yeah man. Somethin' like that. You know everybody got secrets. And Professor Vallone, he like a walkin' secret," said Henry. Just then Gilberto rose, gathered his books, and left the room as quietly as he had come. He hadn't been in class more than five minutes. He must have been taking Vinny's death especially hard. Henry paused for a moment and then went on. “And not just his own secret. Folks tell things to undertakers. I bet that dude heard a lot of other folks’ secrets when he was helpin’ them bury their dead.” Henry still sounded matter-of-fact, as if he were droning on about the weather. But suddenly I found it impossible to ignore the two tattoos which hung below his eye like tiny daggers. Today they made everything he said sound ominous. Clearly, Henry knew from secrets.

I reminded them of their assignment and promised that there would be a replacement teacher before too long. “I’m planning to attend Professor Vallone’s viewing and funeral. If anyone here would like to go . . .” I wondered if anyone else appreciated the irony of funeral service education students attending their prof’s wake and funeral.

No one smiled when Alan Weiner interjected, “If we go, do we have to take notes?”

Gilberto had not returned by the time I dismissed the class.

Chapter 3

AUTOPSY: HEAD BASH
KILLED FUNERAL SCION
Local Undertaker Murdered
Corpse Dumped in Canal

An autopsy of the late Vincent Vallone Jr., whose body was found in the Morris Canal last Tuesday, reveals that the popular local undertaker died as a result of blunt trauma to the head. His body had been dumped into the Canal after the fatal injury. The medical examiner places the date of death as the evening of Tuesday, February 6. Police are investigating his murder. . . .

Before Sol moved in, when the kids were in college, I'd gotten used to living alone. It was during this time that I had refined my longtime affinity for the occasional self-directed monologue. After a while I grew to really appreciate myself as a conversational partner. So there I was, sitting in the kitchen, lingering a little longer than usual over my yogurt and tea and talking earnestly to myself. During a lull, I glanced at the *Jersey City Herald*, which I had brought in and absentmindedly unfolded beside my tea mug on the table.

The paper slid to the floor as I cradled my head in my arms over the counter and shuddered. *Blunt trauma to the head.* The ugly phrase reverberated in my brain. Oh my God! Poor Vinny, self-proclaimed wimp, who masked his timidity with humor. How terrifying his last moments must have been. Who would do this to him? Why? As I struggled to come to terms with this new information, I felt beyond tears, in some new territory where colleagues could be bludgeoned to death.

And being alone in this alien place was suddenly intolerable. I desperately needed to hear a voice other than my own. Over forty years ago, when I was in the sixth grade, I found out that a boy I had an enormous crush on had invited Madeline Millstcin to a Saturday-afternoon movie. In less time than it took to say "Eddie Fisher loves Debbie Reynolds," I had called my best friend for support. And Cindy came through. I still remember what she said: "What'd he do that for, the dumb jerk? You're ten times nicer and prettier than she is." Ever since then I have viewed the telephone as a source of comfort. I would call Illuminada and then Betty. As I extended my hand to pick up the receiver, the phone rang.

It was Illuminada. She didn't even say good morning or apologize for calling before eight. "*Como mierda*, Bel! Did you see today's paper? Vinny Vallone was murdered!"

"I just saw it. I was about to call you. I can't believe it. . . ."

"Well, *chiquita*, you better believe it. Listen, I work for a living, so I don't have time to talk, especially if

I want to go to the viewing. You're going, aren't you?"

Illuminada was always in a hurry now. Her agency had grown since, together with our friend Betty Ramsey, we'd fingered the murderers of RECC's first woman president, Dr. Altagracia Garcia. Now Illuminada Gutierrez, PI, handled more than just child-support collection. She got work from women politicians who wanted to get the dirt on their opponents, from women business owners who suspected pilfering, from divorce lawyers, and from lawyers trying sexual harrassment cases. Illuminada had also developed expertise in a new area called Threat Management so she could protect people from stalkers and kidnappers. In fact, she had so much business that she had hired a few part-time employees to do some of the fieldwork.

But, like Vinny, Illuminada still made time to adjunct at RECC as a way of repaying the community college system that had been there when she herself had needed it. I knew Illuminada would make time for Vinny's viewing, so I was prepared when she offered, "You want me to pick you up? We can go together."

I welcomed the thought of company, especially Illuminada's. I wasn't squeamish about being in close proximity to coffins or corpses either, for that matter, but the sight of grieving relatives always reduces me to tears, even if I don't know them. The fact that Vinny's mother had not lived to learn of her son's "bludgeoning" flashed through my mind, along with pictures of Mark on an Israeli bus. . . . The necessity of responding to Illuminada ended that recurring fantasy. "Sure. Maybe some students will join us. They loved him. I expect a big turnout from RECC, actually." No sooner had I put down the phone than it rang again.

"May I speak with Professor Bel Barrett, please?" The voice on the other end of the line was low and sonorous. The hair on the back of my neck rose. It couldn't be a telemarketer at this hour, could it?

Just to play it safe, I replied in my most hostile tone, "This is she." I waited for the spiel, my stock refusal burning the tip of my tongue and my arm poised to slam down the receiver.

"Pastor Martin Johnson here of Renewal Pentacostal Church. Please forgive me for calling so early, but I wanted to reach you before you left for class. I'd like to make an appointment to see you about one of your students." He paused to give me time to consider.

It was an unorthodox request, but not an unreasonable one. Many of my students had very close ties with their religious groups. I reached across the table for my purse and extricated my date book. He agreed to meet me at the RIP diner later that week. Even with Wendy, my office mate, away on sabbatical, the cubicle we shared was too small and crowded to easily accommodate conferences. I carefully noted our projected appointment, knowing that, if I didn't record it, in a few minutes I might not recall having made it. It wasn't until I put my date book back in my purse that I realized that I hadn't remembered to ask Pastor Johnson which of my one hundred or so students he wanted to see me about.

As I did whenever I was feeling vulnerable—and flashes of someone bashing in my colleague's skull were making me feel very vulnerable—I stashed a small package of M&M's in my purse. Then, remembering a maxim of my mother's, "The worse things are, the better you should look," I decided to really dress for Vinny's viewing.

Vinny had often complimented me on my earrings. I am partial to crafted whimsical pieces that, I hope, distract people from my ummanageable hair, now streaked with gray, and my penchant for loose, comfortable shirts, big bulky sweaters, and even looser and more comfortable jeans. On even the most festive occasions, I wear a lot of black. Rebecca labels my look as hopelessly "sixties meets Soho," and despairs. But in memory of Vinny, I made an effort and chose the earrings Sol bought me last summer at the Lincoln Center Crafts Fair, tiger's-eye entwined in macramé. Then I pulled on a black chenille sweater and a long, black skirt.

Vallone and Sons funeral parlor is imposing in its simplicity. The building had originally been a house, and over the years the Vallone family had enlarged it to accommodate their growing business. But it still looked and felt like a home where mourners were treated like extended family as they said good-bye to their loved ones. As Vinny had been wont to say with barely muted pride, Vallone's offers the last word in "grief management."

The scents of hundreds of carnations, roses, and mums blended into a heady floral effusion that nearly overwhelmed us as we entered the crowded viewing room, stomping the snow off our boots. Illuminada pointed toward a line near the door, and we took our places at the end, joining the people paying their respects to Vinny's family. As if on cue, Alan Weiner and Joevelyn Tate joined us. Alan looked somber in a dark suit and tie. I realized this was the first time I'd seen Alan without his baseball cap. Beneath her feathered felt hat, Joevelyn's face was streaked with tears.

No sooner had I introduced Illuminada to Alan and Joevelyn than Alan began a kind of running commentary. "It looks like they had to do a wax restoration. I mean after being in the river so long and all. . . ."

Joevelyn provided the Greek chorus. Every time the narrator paused for effect, she intoned, "Oh, Jesus, who thought I'd ever see this day?"

As if inspired by her imprecation, Alan continued: "I talked to one of the staff. More than two days in the river and a body's not viewable. Unless the water is below freezing, which it wasn't last week." He stopped for breath.

Joevelyn was right on time, now almost chanting, "Oh, Lord, watch over Professor Vallone."

The expression on my face that greeted Alan's last remark prompted him to quickly add, "Don't worry. They just do the face. That's 'cause the rest of the body is hidden by clothes. And they always use gloves on the hands." Alan paused for breath. I struggled to keep myself from muzzling his mouth with my hand. I regretted not doing so when, mistaking my silence for interest, Alan went on. "A good restorative artist can capture the likeness of the deceased's face. Professor Vallone is very lifelike. You'll see, Professor Barrett. At least it wasn't summer, because in warm weather there are crabs in the Hudson. . . ."

Joevelyn's voice seemed louder now. "Yes, Lord, he with You now." She might have been trying to drown out Alan's relentless retreat into information. I was relieved to note that she seemed to be on good terms with the deity.

I left it to Illuminada to engage Alan in conversation while I stared around the room at the floral offerings. There were two huge open books, the pages of one created entirely of white mums and the words, "Vincent Vallone Jr., beloved colleague, teacher, and friend, from the RECC Adjunct Faculty" written with yellow blossoms. There was another enormous heart crafted of literally hundreds of tiny red and white roses with the simple words, "Vincent Vallone Jr., beloved brother, partner, friend." And right next to it on a stand was a smaller heart made of pink rosebuds with white letters reading, "I love you Uncle Vinny." Everywhere I looked, flowers spoke eloquently of loss. On a tape, Bette Midler intoned "The Wind Beneath My Wings," an elegy in song.

As I scanned the room, I felt a chill. Was Vinny's killer among the viewers? Before I could dwell on that possibility, Amado approached the coffin, knelt, and made the sign of the cross. Like many in the room, he held a rosary, which he brought to his lips. He lingered a moment, crossed himself again, stood, and stepped aside.

Behind him was the unmistakable bulk of Arthur Hoffman, a student I'd had in Speech class a couple of semesters ago. I hadn't known he was in the FSE Program. With his stammer, it was hard to imagine Arthur facilitating funeral arrangements. Arthur had always wanted to be a fireman. But students changed their goals all the time. Perhaps he planned to work in pick up and delivery or embalming, where he wouldn't have too much unscripted contact with the public. With a cursory look at the casket, Arthur bowed his head and moved on after Amado.

Watching them, I realized yet again how frequently community college teaching offers one a real chance to make a difference. Vinny Vallone really had been "the wind beneath the wings" of quite a few people. Thanks to his vision and perseverance, students like Amado and Joevelyn and the others now had the chance to join the ranks of a thriving and useful profession and so to become middle class, a goal they aspired to with almost frightening fervor.

My reverie was interrupted by the sight of Henry Granger, for once, looking appropriately grim in a black overcoat and a gray fedora. He hovered at the edge of the crowd for a moment and then slipped into the line of mourners waiting to approach the coffin. He barely nodded a greeting when he caught my eye and immediately lowered his head. Vinny had never had a chance to apologize to Henry. I could do that for him though. I would schedule a conference with Henry and tell him of Vinny's change of heart about "Gangsta Grief."

When I spotted the familiar figure of our good friend Betty Ramsey behind Henry, I nudged Illuminada and tilted my head in Betty's direction. Betty's new 'do, a halo of coiled dreads, framed her round face. We'd have to get together soon. It had been too long since the three of us had really talked.

Betty was standing next to Father Santos. I recalled the dignity and sense of spirituality he'd brought to the memorial service for Dr. Garcia, the late RECC president, and felt somehow reassured. Betty was probably here representing the current RECC president, Dr. Ron Woodman, who was attending a conference on community college governance in Kentucky.

Betty flashed me a quick, warm smile before resuming her usual no-nonsense expression. After the murder of Altagracia Garcia, a grieving and embittered Betty had toyed with the notion of leaving

RECC. But her idealism had triumphed. So when Dr. Woodman, a newcomer to the infamous political snake pit that is RECC's home turf, begged her to stay, Betty had agreed. She now served as executive assistant to the Nebraska native. Needless to say, he was like the proverbial putty in Betty's managerial hands. Without her he couldn't find the men's room. Hell, to hear Betty tell it, half the time he didn't even know he needed to go.

Behind Betty stood Hattie Majors. I was surprised to see her there until I reminded myself that as the FSE counselor, she would be required to make an appearance. Beneath her burgundy wool turban, Hattie's eyes blinked and the left side of her mouth twitched. Vinny might be dead, but Hattie Majors was condemned to live on as "Batty Hattie" at RECC. I wondered if she had figured this out. Hattie shifted her large frame from side to side as the line of mourners snaked slowly among the blossoms.

A sharp poke in my back, courtesy of Illuminada, jolted me back to the viewing. We had reached the casket. I glanced at the sculpted facsimile of my friend Vinny on a bed of cream-colored satin. Just as Alan had said, someone—perhaps Vinny's brother Victor—had reshaped the corpse's water- and rock-ravaged features into a waxen likeness of Vinny so that we viewers would have something recognizable to mourn.

But that's what it was, a thing, a waxwork with detail worthy of Madame Tussaud, but without life, without soul. I quickly shut my eyes so that the molded effigy would not displace my own recollection of Vinny's face. When I opened them, I saw Gilberto Hernandez, standing like a sentry at the foot of the coffin. His handsome features were immobile, almost as if the same wax worker had molded them in place.

Illuminada and I made our way over to a corner of the room, where Victor Vallone was accepting condolences. He was a rugged-looking man of about forty-five, the older brother. Like Vinny, he had neatly trimmed brown hair that threatened to curl over the part, blue eyes, and a vaguely aquiline nose. But Victor was lean and lanky, unlike Vinny, whose predilection for pasta and sweets had rendered him perennially pudgy. Victor Vallone's face was gaunt and ashen. He'd probably worked late modeling the features of his brother in wax. Victor's own features looked frozen. His eyes were unreadable. Vinny's facial expressions had always been an accurate reflection of his emotional state. Apparently, this was not a family trait.

Standing next to Victor Vallone, her hand clasped in his, was a girl of about nine. Her prepubescent angularity and vaguely aquiline nose marked her as his daughter, the niece Vinny used to brag about whenever I bragged about my kids. Of course, I couldn't remember her name to save myself, so I said, "You must be Vinny's niece. I'm his friend Bel Barrett. Your Uncle Vinny and I used to teach together at the community college. And this is another friend of your uncle's from the college. Her name is Illuminada Gutierrez." I turned and gestured in the direction of Illuminada.

I bumbled on, looking at both the haggard, blank-eyed man and the child. "I'm terribly sorry about what happened to Vinny. He was a wonderful teacher." Feeling my eyes fill and hearing my voice break, I moved away before either Victor or the girl could reply. Waving a quick good-bye to Alan and Joevelyn, who were still behind us, I left the funeral parlor. Betty gave my arm a comforting squeeze as I brushed past her. Hattie Majors lowered and then raised her head in an appropriately somber nod of recognition.

To: Bbarrett@circle.com
From: lbickf@aol.com
Date: 02/13/96 03:28:16

Well, well, well Bbarrett, I bet you never thought the old man had it in him to learn how to use this new gizmo. And thanks to you and Sol for giving me the AOL membership for my birthday. Another *altecocker* I met at shul here came over and showed me how to get it all logged up on your old computer, so here I am.

Your mother and I got a card from Mark the other day. Your mother has it now on the fridge next to the picture of him and Rebecca. Speaking of your mother. Maybe she is finally getting used to the walker. That's good because her knee isn't getting any better. She hasn't been getting out to play bridge much lately, but she sees a few people. The woman next door wants her to read to the blind.

So when are you coming down?

Love,
Pop

Finding my dad's e-mail message after Vinny's viewing had been a jolt. Picturing my eighty-five-year-old father pecking away at the keyboard with his index finger and mastering the intricacies of cyberspace brought new tears to my eyes. It wasn't hard to read between the lines. Ma's arthritis was worse. When had the walker become a necessity? And Sadie Bickoff without a card game was unthinkable. I had come very close to being delivered on a bridge table by the wife of an obstetrician. Why wouldn't Ma have the damn knee surgery already? God, that woman was stubborn.

Suddenly I wanted to see my parents, if only to scold and interfere, which is what Ma always accuses me of whenever I suggest anything. I wouldn't wait for Sol's unpredictable return to visit them. Who knew how much time they had left? I reached for the phone and booked a round-trip flight to Charleston for the weekend after next.

Just as I put down the phone, it rang. "Hello beautiful. How are you? I miss you." Sol sounded so far away, his rich, mellow voice muffled by transatlantic static. He was fine. Tom Minkus and the other American business types Sol was hoping to persuade to invest in public utilities in Prague were enthusiastic. Sol had masterminded the arrangement of a series of meetings with Vaclav Grulich, Czech minister of the interior. Vaclav had a proposal for the Americans to look at. Of course Tom had to tweak Vaclav's proposal a little first, but this time Tom was definitely interested. And of course, as Sol put it, "The bad news is I just can't say when we'll close. It could be in one week or it could be several weeks." Even so, just hearing Sol's voice was a high. Before I got too excited, I made a point of checking my date book to see that

I had marked in a meeting Sol had asked me to attend in his place. I had. Now I just had to remember to check the date book as the days passed. The meeting of Sol's precious Citizens' Coalition to Preserve the Waterfront was over a week away.

It was only after I put down the phone and was dressing for Vinny's funeral that I realized that I hadn't even mentioned Vinny's death to Sol. One of Sol's many virtues is that he appreciates most of my friends, unlike Lenny, my ex, who thought Wendy was "shrill" and called Marilyn "tight-assed" to her face. Sol hadn't known Vinny very well, but the two men had hit it off when they met. I remembered them exchanging amiable barbs over beer and burgers in our postage-stamp–size backyard in Hoboken early last fall. Sol would be horrified to learn that Vinny had been murdered. In a way, I was almost glad I'd forgotten to tell him. Sol was under such pressure to broker this deal. If and when they closed, he'd be handsomely rewarded. The bad news could wait.

A little later that morning, I brushed big, white, wet flakes off my coat and wondered how long it would be before I could dig my car out from under the snow dune covering it. Thanks to the PATH train, I'd been able to get to Jersey City and keep my appointment with Pastor Johnson. This winter had been the snowiest in decades, and it wasn't over yet. I had shoveled the walk and steps in front of our house at least six times in the last week. The once pretty white stuff sure had gotten old fast.

As I was removing my wet gloves and scarf at the RIP Diner, I realized that I had no idea how I would recognize the pastor unless he wore his collar. I ordered my tea, planning to intercept the first man I saw in clerical garb.

"Professor Barrett? I hope you haven't been waiting long. Martin Johnson here." I recognized his voice right away.

Pastor Johnson had escaped my notice, perhaps because his scarf, upturned coat collar, and electric blue earmuffs were an effective disguise. He was a light-skinned African-American man with hazel eyes and a warm, expansive manner. I figured him to be about fifty. After he had hung up his wet coat, I extended my hand in greeting and said, "No. I just got here. How did you know who I was?"

"Your student told me to look for 'a tall white lady with "bad" earrings who wears her eyeglasses on a chain around her neck.' And here you are." Pastor Johnson smiled engagingly, gestured to our waitress for coffee, and settled himself opposite me in the booth.

Amused by his candor, I fingered my earrings. Showers of stones, gleaming black, of course, dangled at least two inches below my still frozen earlobes. I guess they *were* "bad."

"I pray we're not going to get more snow. What do you think?" I queried, hoping some small talk would smooth our transition from strangers to collaborators, pooling our perspectives to help a student.

I must have looked really worried, because he said, "I'm one of those nuts who thinks this snow makes even Jersey City look lovely. But don't worry, we won't be long."

"Thank you." Feeling reassured by what sounded like a sensible agenda, I got right to it. "So tell me, Pastor Johnson, which of my approximately one hundred students did you want to speak to me about? When you called, I had just read that a colleague had been murdered. I was so upset that I forgot to ask you."

"I assume you're referring to Vincent Vallone Jr., the undertaker who taught at RECC? I know he worked closely with you, and I offer you my condolences."

I was beginning to feel just the tiniest bit uncomfortable over the fact that Pastor Johnson seemed to know a lot about me, but I still had no clue as to why he had wanted to meet with me so badly that he walked nearly a mile in the early stages of a blizzard. I nodded in acknowledgment of his offer of sympathy, and he continued.

"You know, Professor Barrett, over the years, quite a few members of our church have taken courses at RECC. So I've heard a lot of things about the college. But it was something that I heard about you in particular that made me pick up the phone and call you." When I furrowed my brow and glanced at my watch, he smiled and said, "Okay, I said I'd be brief, and I will. 'You're not in the pulpit now' is what my wife always tells me when I start running on." In a lower voice, he said, "I know you had a lot to do with helping to figure out who really murdered that woman president they had at RECC, even though you didn't take the credit. I heard all about it."

Uh-oh. I felt my stomach tighten just a little. An expression Mark used whenever I brought up a topic he didn't want to address flashed through my mind: *Let's not go there.* Something in my gut told me I didn't want to go where Pastor Johnson was heading.

"So I wanted to see you about Henry Granger."

I nodded again, somehow not too surprised. I knew Henry was active in a church, I just hadn't remembered which one. Pastor Johnson was fully launched into his narrative now. "The night before I called you, Henry's grandmother, Pearl Hoskins, came to see me. She was very distraught." The Pastor paused briefly before going on. "It seems the police came to her place, where Henry lives, and questioned him about Mr. Vallone's murder." Pastor Johnson lowered his head, and when he lifted it, he looked older than he had before he sat down. He seemed out of steam.

"Why do they suspect Henry?" Before the words had left my lips I realized how naive my question was in light of Henry's telling tattoos. But it wouldn't hurt to sound naive. Perhaps I'd learn something. After all, most of what I knew about Henry's background was based on rumor and conjecture.

"Professor Barrett, Henry Granger is a paroled ex-convict with two homicides on his record and no alibi for the approximate time of Vincent Vallone's death." Pastor Johnson was looking directly at me as he spoke, confirming both rumors and conjecture in one stark sentence. "He claims he acted in self-defense in both those homicides. He belonged to a gang then, and he did a lot of things. . . ." Pastor Johnson's voice trailed off. The lines crinkling the corners of his eyes seemed to have multiplied in the last five minutes. "I understand," he said, his voice wearier, more resigned, "I understand that the police have to investigate every lead, but Henry's grandmother doesn't believe Henry killed Vincent Vallone. "And," he added firmly, "I don't either."

Before I could utter so much as one word, Pastor Johnson put his hand up in a gesture that stifled even *my* impulse to respond, and continued speaking in a low, urgent tone. "You don't have to say anything right now. In fact, I don't want you to. I want you to take plenty of time to think about what I'm going to ask you."

Pastor Johnson's eyes locked on mine. "I promised Pearl Hoskins I'd try to help Henry. Henry thinks that a disagreement he had with Professor Vallone—something about a grade—is going to be turned into a motive. You know how it is. The police have no other leads, so because of his record and, you know, because of how things are racially, Henry's sure he's going to end up being arrested for this murder."

The pastor drained the last of his coffee and put his cup down. "Pearl Hoskins is a determined woman. She went to a lawyer, and he told her to hire a private investigator because, until they actually arrest Henry, there's nothing a lawyer can do. You know, Professor Barrett, that lawyer charged Pearl Hoskins over a hundred dollars just to tell her that." He shook his head in disbelief. "So Pearl went to the private investigator the lawyer named, and his rates were very high too, almost as bad as the lawyer's. Professor Barrett, she just hasn't got that kind of money. And the church . . ." He snorted. "We don't have it either. No way." He shook his head again. "But the investigator mentioned your name. Said he thought you might be able to help her. Seems you've got quite a few fans out there, Professor." I swear, as he said this his eyes burned into mine. "So here I am, asking you to find out what you can about who really killed Vincent Vallone, so Henry doesn't have to go back to jail."

My stomach was doing a good imitation of a pretzel by the time the pastor finished his last sentence. The man must be a demon in the pulpit. Before I could open my mouth to speak, he stood, put a five-dollar bill on the table, and said quietly, "Just think about it. That's all I'm really asking. And then—his voice was a murmur now—"please let me know what decision your conscience guides you to." Having thrown down that guilt-inducing gauntlet, he placed his card on the table in front of me.

Right then was when I should have said, "No. Thank you very much. I no longer involve myself in what should be police work. Been there. Done that. Over. Finito." But I didn't.

"Now let's see what new wonders the good Lord has wrought outside. Look, it's still coming down." His hard work over, Pastor Johnson spoke matter-of-factly now. We held coats for each other and, buttoning up, made our way wordlessly into the street, where newly fallen flakes had, in fact, blanched the mounds of dirt-covered snow.

I hoped a few hours at school catching up on committee work and reading student papers would calm me. Frankly, the thought of Henry Granger going to jail for a crime I was pretty sure he hadn't committed triggered my lifelong urge to do what I could to even the metaphorical playing field that was America. That was why, in the sixties, I'd marched, protested, registered voters, hugged trees, circulated petitions, and burned underwear. And that was why I taught at RECC. But the sixties had been over for a long time. And now that I was a fifty-something, estrogen-enhanced wanna-be grandmother, what could I possibly do?

For starters, I could deny the whole problem. And that's what I tried to do by burying myself in the familiar but always engaging stories that my students told in their essays. So eager was I to get to my desk that I almost didn't mind climbing the six flights of stairs to my floor. The elevators in the decrepit former office building that housed the RECC English Department were notoriously unreliable. The only thing you could count on them to do was get stuck. Maria Alcenan had delivered her baby, Rosario Felice, waiting for the repairmen between the eighth and ninth floors.

I was grateful for the fire exits, steep stairwells appended to two corners of the building. I didn't care that these cinder-block canyons were so cold that only the most desperate and furtive of RECC's outcast smokers frequented them. Even so, the stairwells were an inviting alternative to the elevators. Besides, so much regular exercise had to be good for me.

So I thought, as, breathing hard, I approached the third floor. I smelled cigarette smoke just before a shadow glided between me and the overhead light. On the landing loomed a dark silhouette. My rib cage contracted. I tightened my grip on the banister and pressed on, peering upward. The menacing figure moved, blocking my passage. Above me stood a man, a curl of cigarette smoke circling his head.

"Yo, Professor." Henry Granger's basso voice was uncharacteristically brittle.

"Oh Henry, it's you. I was scared for a minute."

"Why ain't you still scared? You here by yourself wit a ex-con, a murder suspect," Henry snarled. He deliberately dropped his cigarette to the cement floor and ground it under his heel. From where I stood on the stairs, I was eye level with his fists. I watched them clenching and unclenching.

The times Henry and I had conferred over his speeches last semester flashed through my head. The angry young man towering above me seemed like a different person, barely polite. My stomach churned as I struggled to recall the Henry I knew. Ignoring his self-deprecating outburst and his bad-boy posturing, I cracked, "Yeah, Henry. I'm just terrified," hoping to get a smile out of him. "Actually, I'm glad I ran into you. You're on my top Post-it, see?" I pulled a pad of lavender Post-its out of my purse.

Students refer to me as "Professor Post-it" because I'm so memory-challenged that I rely almost totally on Post-its to keep track of my commitments. "Look, the top one has your name on it. I was going to call you to make an appointment."

"Why you got my name on that paper?" He glanced down at the ridiculous purple square I waved at him like an olive branch.

"Well, Henry, what I wanted to talk to you about is this." I actually had to twist my neck around and up to see Henry's face. "Professor Vallone was planning to apologize to you for his initial reaction to your research paper topic. He misunderstood what you are trying to do in the paper. He said as soon as he realized this, he regretted giving you an F on your outline and telling you your topic was inappropriate and that you had to choose another one. . . ."

Henry pursued his own agenda. "He tell you what the cops got to say about me walkin' outta his class? A lotta students saw me. I tol' a lot of them how that fat-ass white faggot dissed me and my work. Man, I even tol' the counselor." From my vantage point on the steps below I once again became aware of Henry's fists clenching and unclenching just inches from my head. "Man, if I *was* gonna do him, I woulda done him right then." Henry's words echoed in the stone stairwell long after he himself had passed through the door to the third floor.

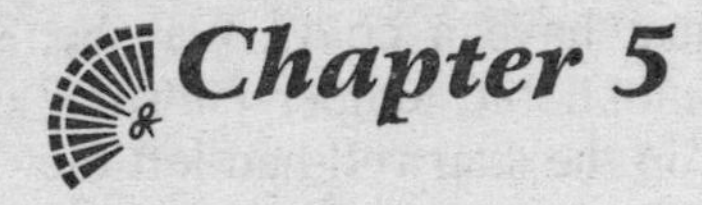

Chapter 5

To: Hattie Majors, Counselor FSE
From: Bel Barrett
Re: Eleanor Chambers
Date: February 15, 1996

Hattie, since I've no more copies of the referral forms and you haven't sent me the replacement forms I requested, I assume you're out of them too. At any rate, attached is a list of students who have missed more than three classes. Of particular concern is Eleanor Chambers who has already missed five classes in "Funeral Service History: Writing and Research" this semester. Please let me know what you turn up about her.

I myself had a week's worth of work to get done and only a day to do it. The dean had sent word that he'd finally found someone to take over the class Vinny had co-taught with me as well as the one Vinny had taught at night. Even so, I was up to my earrings in unread papers, so I planned to retreat to my office after class, to read and respond to the piles of essays and speech outlines that covered my desk.

But first there was class. Henry Granger did not

show up. This worried me because he had not missed a class all semester. Had the police inquiry into his whereabouts on the night of the murder totally unhinged him? Or did he just have a cold? Was he, perhaps, regretting his homophobic temper tantrum? Frankly, Henry's outburst on the stairwell had left me anxious and confused.

But there was no time to think longer about Henry just then, because Joevelyn came in with Tamisha, her four-year-old daughter. "Sorry Professor Barrett, but Tamisha, she with me again today. The baby-sitter's kids all sick, so I don't want her there. I hope you don't mind none. She not gonna be no trouble, right Tamisha?" Joevelyn gave the little girl a timeless look that said, "You'd better be good or else." Tamisha nodded vigorously, her tiny braids bobbing. My inner grandmother wanted to settle her on my lap. Instead, I unloaded my books onto the desk.

"Look. I got me a book too," Tamisha boasted, waving her coloring book and offering it to me to examine.

I stooped to look. There was Barney, crayoned a regal purple. "Mmm. I like the color you chose for Barney, Tamisha. Now we're going to start our class. Do you want to sit next to Mommy, or here near the window where you can see out?" Suddenly shy, Tamisha darted to Joevelyn's side and crawled into her lap. I helped Tamisha into the seat next to her mother, and Joevelyn handed her a pink plastic bookbag filled, I hoped, with art supplies, paper, and picture books. A quick survey of faces revealed that Eleanor Chambers was yet again among the missing.

"There will be a new instructor taking over Professor Vallone's part of this course. He'll begin next week." I paused. It seemed appropriate to begin our transition to a Vinny-less class in silence. Then, taking a deep breath, I continued. "I'd like to begin today with questions you may have about your research. How's it going? Are you having any problems? Yes, Alan?"

"I'm researching Jewish funeral traditions in the Diaspora and I found lots of information on the Internet." Alan smiled, pleased with his accomplishment. "Is it necessary to use other sources as well?" He said "other sources" dismissively, seduced by the instant gratification awaiting travelers on the information highway.

"There are several factors to consider here, Alan . . ." I began.

"I wanna drink, Mama." Tamisha's stage whisper persisted until Joevelyn managed to extricate a bottle of juice from her purse and hand it to the child, who took a few sips and resumed coloring, her features knotted in concentration.

"Why they don't let us take the books out of the library at least for overnight? Now I got to pay the baby-sitter not just for when I'm in classes, but for when I be at the library too." Joevelyn's question sounded like a whine until I reminded myself what little time she'd spent in libraries. While I explained again about the reserve system, I mused for the umpteenth time on the fact that higher education was originally designed for the sons of the leisure classes—free spirits unfetterd by jobs and child care.

"Mama! I gotta go pee-pee." Urgency heightened Tamisha's stage whisper this time and drew my attention to her juice bottle. Predictably, it was empty. With an audible sigh of resignation, Joevelyn rose and, taking the little girl's hand, led her from the room.

"What do you do if an article's long? Xerox the whole thing? That's a whole lotta dimes, man." It was Gilberto, sounding petulant. At first glance he looked uncharacteristically ordinary in jeans and a faded sweatshirt. Then I noticed his left eye, a slit in a swollen purple smear. The classic shiner made a mockery of the chiseled perfection of the rest of his face. No wonder Gilberto sounded down.

"Yeah. And what if you Xerox an article and then you don't even use it? That happened to me with two articles so far. Like you said last week, everything we read's not gonna be useful." Even Amado sounded cranky.

As I explained the logistics of library research, I fumbled in my purse for my supply of dry-erase markers and found two: one black, the other red. Then I approached Tamisha, who had returned from the bathroom and was rocking back and forth in her seat and looking around the room. "Tamisha, would you like to draw on the board?" I drew a smiley face with the red marker. Soon Tamisha was perched on a chair facing the board and sketching a red flower with a black stem. Or was it a red tree with a black trunk? Or maybe a red balloon with a black string?

After class I went straight to my office. I had been cloistered there reading papers for several hours when I heard a knock on my door. I leaned over to open it and was surprised to see a tall, thin African-American woman with steel gray hair. She was a stranger to me. "Yes. May I help you?" I figured she was looking for someone, and I could direct her.

"Professor Barrett? I'm looking for Professor Barrett." I was really annoyed at the interruption. I had made great strides and could even imagine finishing all but one set of speech outlines by late afternoon.

"I'm Professor Barrett. What may I do for you?" I stood and extended my hand in welcome to the woman who was intruding on my precious time.

"Pearl Hoskins here." The name sounded familiar. Where had I heard it? Was she an adjunct? Taking in my puzzled look, the woman spoke again. "Henry Granger's grandmother. I'm sorry to come barging in here without calling."

"Oh, of course, Pastor Johnson mentioned you the other day. Let me take your coat." I gestured toward Wendy's empty chair.

"No thank you." Pearl Hoskins remained standing and kept her coat buttoned, so I didn't sit either. Two tall women face to face, we nearly filled the cubicle, "Look Professor, I can see you're busy, so I'll say what I came to say." My visitor inhaled sharply and began. "I'm not one to ask for no favors. I'm an LPN and pretty much retired now. I work hard all my life. Never spent a dime I didn't earn. Never asked for nothin' before this. But I don't want to see my only grand go to jail again. He done paid his dues. You got kids, I see." Her gray eyes had lighted on a snapshot on my bookshelf of Mark and Rebecca laughing at the camera.

Pearl Hoskins didn't wait for me to respond. She hurried on, her words racing after each other, her breath short, almost as if she were running. "Henry, he my daughter's boy. She gone. AIDS took her when Henry was ten." She glanced away for a moment but continued to speak. "Henry's father, he in jail. Henry don't know him, never knowed him. So after Serena passed, her boy come to live with me. Lord have mercy—Henry, he sure was wild then." Pearl Hoskins shook her head as if still amazed at Henry's youthful wildness. "Got in with a gang in Currie Woods, where we live, you know, the projects." I did indeed know Currie Woods, your generic crime- and drug-infested inner-city housing project. "Went to jail when he was really still a baby. But there was a purpose. 'Cause in prison Henry find Christ. He saved now." She paused here for breath, but also to lower her head for a second or two, a private moment of pure thanksgiving.

"Henry, he wid me again now, and this time I don't want to lose him. He got a future now. I couldn't help him before, couldn't seem to get through. But now he older and he find Christ. I thought if I come to see you, talked to you myself, maybe . . ." With great effort, Pearl Hoskins stopped talking, stood perfectly still for a moment, and then said plainly, "Please help me save my grand. And now I done said my piece, I will be leavin'. I thank you for your time, Professor." And leave she did. A small puddle where she had stood—snow melting off her boots—was the only proof that Pearl Hoskins had been there at all.

I dropped into my chair, stunned by the power of the woman's stark narrative. Her simple words traveled the path already smoothed by Pastor Johnson's oratory. How agonizing it must be to lose a daughter, to watch her waste away, enduring the particular horror of an AIDs death. And how could one bear to know one's orphaned grandbaby had killed? Was in prison?

As a mother who lived and breathed in anticipation of the day I would become a grandmother—

an honest-to-God, stroller-pushing, diaper-changing, cookie-making, reading-aloud grandmother—I could not fit Pearl Hoskin's experiences into my images of grandmotherhood. As I was replaying her visit in my mind, I knew I would try to figure out who really killed Vinny.

Chapter 6

Teaching Journal

Vincent Vallone Jr.
January 29–February 2, 1996

Monday's class was over-the-top. I was totally prepared and the students absolutely adored the mummy slides I showed. I know they'd love a field trip to the Egyptian wing of the Met. We just have to take them. Everyone seemed really wrapped up in the subject and there was no "dead" time (Just making sure you're paying attention, Bel!).

But today, three people came in late: Joevelyn, Amado, and, would you believe, Alan. They were all over fifteen minutes late. What's a poor adjunct to do? Would they do that if I were full-time? And they always have a totally professor-proof excuse. The baby-sitter didn't show, the bus didn't stop, their boss wouldn't let them out of work on time, their car was broken into, they had to go to court, or—don't forget this one,

Bel—they had to take a dying relative to the ER. I know you say a lot of the time they really can't help it, but their tardiness absolutely destroys me. I'm not used to it. Very few people are late for funerals.

But that's not the worst thing. I'm totally terrified. One of our students is following me around, and another wants to kill me. . . .

When I finished reading Vinny's journal, I felt so down. I could just hear him. It was so hard to believe that he wouldn't ever again stick his head into my office to say hello and tell me an awful joke. I resolved to take the FSE class to the Met myself. And I would also contact Eleanor Chambers too and see if I could get her to return to class.

As I sat in my kitchen, holding those yellow sheets of paper covered in Vinny's slanted scrawl, I realized that my career as a graduate student in English Education and Applied Linguistics at Eleanor Roosevelt University might very well have died with Vinny. I was taking only one course, the seminar in classroom research, but without an ongoing teaching journal to analyze for my final project, I was in big trouble. To make matters worse, I had missed a seminar session the week that I'd had to prepare material to teach while covering Vinny's section, and I was also way behind in the reading. I could not bear to think about the demise of my long-postponed graduate studies just then.

Vinny's funeral was a blur, albeit a long blur, in a packed church redolent with the heavy scent of flowers. They overflowed the open space between the altar and the pews, making a bright backdrop for the casket. Saint Anselmo's was well heated against the cold, unusual even for February. I sat crammed into a pew between Illuminada and Alan Weiner, without even enough room to wriggle out of my coat. I groped in my purse for my fan, which I still carried, even though I hadn't much use for it since I'd begun hormone replacement therapy. From where we were sitting, I could not see Victor Vallone or his daughter, but I imagined them in the front rows, still numbed by their loss and by the brutal act that had caused it.

Father Santos conducted the entire Mass, and the distinctive, cloying scent of incense threatened to overpower the aroma of the flowers. Most of my students filed up to the communion rail, while Illuminada, Alan and I remained in our pew nestled in our wet coats. In the pew ahead of us sat Henry Granger. I couldn't see his face, but I wondered what feelings the ceremony evoked in him.

I was aware of Alan turning this way and that while his classmates were taking communion. Suddenly I felt his hand on my arm. "Look, Professor Barrett. See that woman over there?" Turning to follow Alan's pointing finger, I glimpsed Eleanor Chambers sitting across the aisle several rows behind us. "Isn't she in our program? What happened to her? She hasn't been to class in weeks." Wearing a black wool coat still glistening with moisture, Eleanor sat stiffly, her eyes glued to the casket. She wore no hat and her usually dull brown hair gleamed with a halo of melted snow. An arrow of sunlight filtering through the stained glass window tinted her expressionless face a ghostly green.

I knew a message from my maker when I saw one. As sure as God made M&M's and estrogen, that green arrow was pointing at Eleanor, highlighting what I had been trying not to think about ever since I had learned that Vinny had been murdered. Sitting there in church, I realized that I was probably the only person besides Vinny and Eleanor who knew about Eleanor's crush on Vinny. Now Vinny was dead. Had he seen Eleanor after he and I had talked at lunch? Had he discouraged her so adamantly that she'd retaliated by bashing in his skull? Was the tall, awkward, nondescript Eleanor Chambers capable of the hellish fury traditionally attributed to scorned women?

I made a point of walking out of the church behind Eleanor. And when I tapped her on the shoulder and linked arms with her as we left St. Anselmo's, I was more than just a concerned professor. Eleanor had started at the pressure of my hand. "Eleanor," I began. "It's good to see you again. We've missed you in class lately." Eleanor lowered her eyes, but she didn't speak. I persisted, beginning to realize that I might be pretty much on my own in this conversation. "Professor Vallone's death has hit all of us very hard." She lowered her head further, her chin now barely protruding from the watch-plaid scarf at her neck. Turtlelike, she was doing her best to disappear into an invisible shell. "Eleanor, we need to talk. Let's schedule a conference, shall we?" Eleanor managed a barely perceptible nod.

She might very well be just a student poised to drop out of school completely now that her idol was dead. On the other hand, she might be a murderer wary of discovery. How absurd. No wonder I never watch TV. My overworked imagination provides me with entertainment enough, and pretty strong stuff too. My mental picture of Eleanor Chambers, stone-cold killer, vanished as I confronted the mousy woman in front of me.

I pride myself on being able to talk some sense into

would-be dropouts, persuading them to stay in school and earn their degrees. I figured I shouldn't put off a conference with Eleanor, nor rely solely on the dubious talents of Batty Hattie to help her. No way. I should talk to her at once and get her back to class. So I persisted. "Actually, we could even chat a bit now, on the way to the cemetery. Let's sit together on the bus." Vallone and Sons had hired several buses to transport mourners to the nearby cemetery since many, like me, had been forced to leave their snowed-in cars at home.

I interpreted Eleanor's silence as aquiescence, and, taking her firmly by the elbow, edged her onto the bus. There were no seats together, so I maneuvered her into an aisle seat and positioned myself in the one directly across from her. "Eleanor, I'm very concerned about you. So was Professor Vallone," I added, curious to see her reaction. "You've missed a few classes." I did not let on that I knew about her pathetic crush on Vinny. At the mention of his name, Eleanor looked up but didn't break her silence.

"Eleanor." As I spoke her name again, I reached across the aisle and patted her arm, continuing in my most soothing voice. "I assume you've experienced some personal difficulties that have made you miss classes, but I suspect that you have the ability to be a strong student. Professor Vallone thought so too." Again, at the mention of Vinny's name Eleanor's head rose, and I could feel her arm tremble beneath my hand.

"I want you to return to class and to consider seeing a counselor." At this, her lashes flickered above her downcast eyes. Fearing I had blundered, I ad-libbed hastily: "The dean recommmends counseling for all the FSE students who want it. It's part of the grieving process." Some students became irate at the very mention of the word "counselor." And of course, these students were often among our most troubled. Eleanor would probably not avail herself of Hattie Major's services, but I felt I had to make the suggestion. "We're all going to miss Professor Vallone. But we have to go on without him now. He would want that." I saw a tear fall from Eleanor's now rapidly blinking lashes. It glittered on her black coat.

The instant the bus jolted to a halt near the newly dug grave, Eleanor rose, her shoulders hunching up and down. I stood too and, moved by her silent sobs, enfolded the tall, gawky woman, coat and all, in a clumsy hug right there in the aisle of the bus. I felt her stiffen in my arms and then, still wordless, she lifted her shoulders and jerked up her elbows, easily breaking the circle of my embrace. Her face flushed, she turned her head at once and moved toward the door at the front of the bus. Hurrying after her, I watched her walk swiftly along the narrow path in the snow that led to the cemetery gate. I cringed even as I called out to Eleanor's back, "See you in class next week!" in that inane way that some people say, "Have a nice day!" after you have just told them you have cancer.

The day after Vinny's funeral it finally stopped snowing. I suited up in my parka and boots and headed outside to shovel for what seemed like the millionth time. Gradually other shovelers appeared, neighbors on our block of brickfront townhouses all eager to avoid the stigma of a snowy sidewalk, not to mention a lawsuit. We worked in compatible silence, many of us too winded by our exertions to crack more than a smile of resignation.

When I had finally cleared the sidewalk and the

path to the steps, I was out of breath but experiencing a definite endorphin rush. Leaving my boots at the door, I headed inside where it was cozy and warm. I automatically turned on the radio, now permanently set at 1010 WINS. With an ad for snow tires droning in the background, I threw together a melted Swiss cheese and apple sandwich on Hoboken coal-oven whole wheat bread. Virginia Woolf was slinking around my ankles until I sank into my favorite spot on the loveseat to savor my lunch, sip tea, and think. Then the cat leapt into my lap for some serious snoozing.

Snug in my Hoboken haven, I could almost forget that Mark was in danger from suicide bombers and my mom was suffering from crippling arthritis. But I couldn't seem to forget about Vinny's murder. I would have to call Betty and Illuminada. I wonder how they'd react to my getting talked into trying to figure out who really killed him. Whatever they thought, I knew they'd help. Sitting quietly and sipping sherry, I replayed Henry's angry outburst on the stairs. And once again I felt the sudden force with which Eleanor Chambers had broken free of my hug.

". . . The first bomb ripped through a commuter bus during morning rush hour in Jerusalem killing twenty-three people, including two Americans . . ." Swatting a startled Virginia Woolf from my lap, I sped to the phone.

Chapter 7

To: Bbarrett@circle.com
From: Rbarrett@UWash.edu
Date: 02/25/96
Re: Mark

Don't get your underwear in a wad, Mom, Mark's okay. He just called me from the pay phone on the kibbutz after he tried to reach you. He figured you'd lose it as soon as you heard the news, so he phoned. But your phone has been busy and a lot of other people were waiting to call their families, so he laid it on me and then he went to bed. We figured you're trying to phone the kibbutz and that's why your line's been busy for so long. Anyway, I promised him I'd phone you right away, but I can't get through to you either. (Call waiting is very nineties, Mom.)

I don't know if Mark wants me to tell you, so you don't know this, but he's got a girlfriend, Batsheva or something, a native Israeli who was actually born on the kibbutz. She sounds really cool.

My big news is Keith's getting a new bike and giving me his old one. That way we can ride together. Talk to you soon. Relax.

Love,
Rebecca

I finally got through to the kibbutz office's answering machine and its infuriatingly cheerful Hebrew greeting. I never did learn what became of the frantic English message I left on it. After hanging up in frustration, I realized that it was now night in Israel, too late to expect to reach anyone in the kibbutz office. I was trying to make my shaking fingers hit the right keys so I could log on to the *Jerusalem Post*. I had to learn the names of the two Americans who had died in the explosion. Just then, like Mary Poppins with a sherry bottle instead of an umbrella, Betty materialized at my door.

"Lord girl, you're in a state. Here. Drink this, why don't you?" Make no mistake. My friend Betty "Ramrod" Ramsey can be a bossy, take-charge, controlling bitch, but I have learned to love her for it. Within minutes, she had poured me a sherry, settled me on the loveseat out of her way, and begun checking my e-mail. Her fingers ranged calmly over the keyboard, and *voila*, she was on-line. "Mark's fine, Bel. He called your daughter. Here, read this for yourself." As I leaned over the screen, scanning Rebecca's message, waves of relief washed through my body.

I didn't even hear the doorbell chime, but I recognized Illuminada's voice before I saw her dancing up and down to shake the snow off her boots. "*Dios mio!* Enough with this snow already." Looking at my tear-streaked face and then at Betty's grin, she quipped, "So the wake is over, I guess. Mark's okay, right? He called?"

"Mark's just fine. He couldn't get through Bel's communications blackout here, so he called his sister in Seattle, no less. His mom's home chewing her nails and imagining him splattered all over Jerusalem and the dude's not only fine, he's scoring chicks. Wouldn't you know?" Betty sounded relieved too, I thought, in spite of her mocking tone.

Illuminada's delicate features were brightened by her biggest grin. "You know, Bel Barrett, with you, I can never tell what's going on. You cry when you're sad, you cry when you're happy. Lighten up, *chiquita.*"

"Listen, Carmen Miranda, when Luz is two minutes late getting the car back from a trip to the corner store, you're calling the National Guard. Watch who you tell to lighten up."

Illuminada's lips turned up again, testimony to the truth of my words."Yeah, I'm bad, all right. But remember when Randy stayed out all night without calling General Mama Ramsey? And you and I ended up camping out the whole night at Betty's just to keep her from killing the poor *muchacho* when he finally showed up the next morning? That boy owes us." While Illuminada was talking, Betty flipped through my sheaf of take-out menus. In less than half an hour we were slurping from steaming bowls of *Tom Kha Kai*, the Thai version of chicken soup redolent with lemon grass and coconut milk, while cartons of *Mee Grob* and *Pad Ma Keur* stayed warm in the oven.

"So Bel, I keep telling you, more people get killed in traffic accidents every year than by terrorist bombings. I mean you have to shape up and cope. The kid's there for a few more months. The odds are overwhelmingly in favor of his survival. You can't do this to yourself every time there's an incident in the Middle East." It was Illuminada, digesting her dinner and lecturing me as we all relaxed around the kitchen table. Her affinity for reason may be one of the qualities that makes her a great private investigator, but sometimes it drives me crazy.

"You're right. But I have a plan. I know how to protect Mark." I waited for their reaction. It was a short wait.

"You're going to airlift the kid out of Israel and bring him home?" It was Betty, her voice still mocking.

"No, although I wish I could. I wish he'd never gone in the first place, not now . . ."

"So are you going to tell us your plan, or do we just sit here and wait while you go through your whole wish list about how the Israelis and the Palestinians should sit down and work things out so there can be peace?" Illuminada feigned a yawn. Patience has never been her strong suit.

"I'm going to make a bargain with God," I announced. I hadn't planned to put it this way, but I sure had gotten their attention.

"Say what, girl? You're going to do what? I don't think I heard you right." Betty sounded as if I had announced that I was going to dance naked in the snow.

"If I figure out who really killed Vinny, nothing will happen to Mark," I added by way of an admittedly lame explanation.

"*Caramba*, Bel! Now you've really gone off the deep end. I think all that estrogen in that patch you're sitting on has affected your brain." Illuminada sounded really worried.

"No. Listen. One of my students, Henry Granger . . ."

By the time I finished telling them about Henry, Pastor Johnson and Pearl Hoskins, Betty and Illuminada were looking at each other and shaking their heads.

"It's too bad that Henry Granger's nice grandmother has to suffer. But, Bel, he *is* a logical suspect. After all, he does have a record and a motive. There have been several cases of students shooting their profs over grades. But that's neither here nor there. What's all this got to do with Mark? I somehow missed the connection." Illuminada was leaning forward, speaking slowly, as she would to a slightly deaf person or a slow child.

"Hello Bel. Welcome to the real world. Tell your friends what the hell you're talking about." Nobody has ever told Betty that you catch more flies with honey than with vinegar.

"I know someone else with a motive, a stronger one than Henry Granger has," I began.

"For God's sake, Bel. Lots of people might have had motives. Think about it. Batty Hattie has been wishing Vinny dead ever since he rechristened her." Like the good professional she was, Illuminada would think of all the angles. So, of course, she would bring up Hattie.

"Hattie's underqualified and politically connected and she doesn't give a damn about the students, and she hated Vinny, it's true, but do you really think she'd murder him?" I asked.

Betty nodded, and I could see the wheels turning. "She's a spiteful bitch with a mean tongue in her head. Even the president's afraid of her tongue. Who knows? And I heard that Vinny really trashed her all the time . . ." Betty looked thoughtful. "We can't write her off. Let's ask around."

"During my lifetime, Bel. Tomorrow is a work day." Clearly piqued now, Illuminada was tapping her perfectly manicured nails on the table. So I described Eleanor's crush on Vinny, her notes and phone messages, his teaching journal, and my encounter with her after Vinny's funeral. I didn't mention the green arrow of tinted sunlight I had seen pointing at Eleanor during Vinny's funeral mass. They'd lock me up.

"Bel, I see where you're going, and yes, maybe we can look into this a little." Illuminada was intrigued in spite of herself. "I think she's a long shot. But we still have to check her out. And the others too. We owe it to Vinny. God, that man was the Cesar Chavez of adjuncts, the way he helped us to unionize."

"Well, if we're going to do this, we better do it right." When Betty said that, it felt like old times. Sure enough, she was getting out her power notebook and beginning to type. In a minute, I knew, she'd start giving orders. In fact, the very next words out of her mouth were "Bel, you should look into Hattie and Eleanor. . . ."

"Slow down. You know, Vinny had a lot going on in his life outside of RECC. He was a partner in a pretty successful family business. . . ." I wasn't about to let Betty have all the fun.

"And he was gay." It was Illuminada, looking at what she always called "the big picture."

"You know, I should look into the business a little. Talk to the brother," said Betty. I supressed a smile. Betty was even giving orders to herself now. She was too much.

"All this is well and good, but, Bel, what has finding Vinny's killer got to do with Mark? That's what I still don't get." Iluuminada chucked me under the chin with her index finger, the light gesture softening her question.

"You really meant it, didn't you, Bel? Your twisted

postmenopausal mind thinks that if you try to help Henry Granger and his grandmother, God will keep an eye on Mark. That's where you're taking us, isn't it?" It was Betty, matter-of-fact now.

"Something like that," I said simply. Helping Henry and Pearl Hoskins was something I felt I should try to do. Illuminada was doing it "for Vinny." I preferred to help the living. Each to her own, I figured.

"Bel, when was the last time you went to synagogue? You aren't exactly tight with the Lord, you know." Betty, of course, never missed Sunday Mass. She didn't understand how I could consider myself Jewish if I wasn't always sure I believed in God and showed up in synagogue only twice a year. I didn't understand how she could consider herself a feminist and yet live with the Pope's prohibitions against reproductive freedom, women and gays in the priesthood, and gay marriage.

"Forget her relationship with God." With a wave of her small hand, Illuminada dismissed theology. As a reaction against her mother's nearly fanatical piety, Illuminada had embraced atheism. "What about her relationship with Sol? Remember Sol, Bel? That super guy you live with? The one you're always saying is so caring, so funny and smart? That Sol. What about him? He told you he's out of your life if you ever get involved with another murder, Bel. He'll walk."

Illuminada was right. Sol would go nuts. But I had a feeling we would know who Vinny's killer was long before Sol got home.

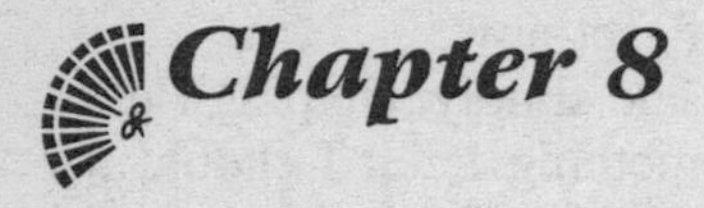

Chapter 8

To: Professor Bel Barret
From: Hattie Majors, Counselor
Funeral Service Education Program
Re: Appropriate referral forms
Date: February 26, 1996

Attached are the appropriate referal forms and the list of students with attendence problems you sent me. I assume that you lost the forms I sent you last week via campus mail. After you have filled out the appropriate forms appropriately, I will attempt to contact the students vis-à-vis there attendence.

When I finally got Hattie's memo, I was so enraged that as soon as I was out of class, I strode the two blocks to her office and rapped hard on the door. If Batty Hattie wanted to play rough . . . I had briefly considered the classic revenge of the English prof, correcting the spelling and word-choice errors in her memo and sending it back, only I was afraid she wouldn't get it. But that's how mad I was. I kept mumbling to myself, *I don't care who her goddamn brother-in-law is either. I have tenure. I belong to a union.* I was so pissed off that I was halfway to the Counseling Center before I remembered that I might be on my way to meet a murderess rather than to dress down a multiply challenged colleague. This realization tempered my approach to Hattie.

As I knocked on her office door, I heard Hattie talking inside. I hoped she wasn't with a student, but I doubted it. Word of her incompetence was out and most RECC students didn't queue up outside her office until they needed her signature to register or add and drop courses.

"No, I bought them both. I'm going to try them both on at home tonight and see which one goes best with my green shoes. I really want to wear those green suede . . ." Hattie was on the phone, probably with her sister, Ms. Commissioner. Somehow that didn't surprise me. I rapped harder, louder. "Damn it. I'll call you later." Her voice changed from buddy-buddy to bureaucrat in the time it took her to put down the phone.

"Come in. Oh. It's you, Bel." Hattie's eyes were blinking and her lips moving jerkily. She was wearing her trademark turban, this one a grayish affair that I guessed was intended to coordinate with her gray power suit. She made a visible effort to recover from her surprise and gestured at the chair opposite her desk. "Have a seat. Didn't you get those referral forms?" She began to rummage through her desk as if looking for more of the damned forms.

"Yes, Hattie. I got your memo and the forms. In fact, that's why I'm here. I wanted to see if you're all right. You're usually so gracious, but you seemed a bit—oh, I don't know—a bit edgy, I guess, in your memo. I figured you must be swamped doing bereavement therapy. So I thought I'd just pop in and see how you're holding up under the deluge."

"Deluge? There's no deluge. I've been saying for years that that slick little weasel was overrated. These students don't give a shit about your precious buddy Vinny Vallone. All they want is their grade and their piece of paper. You don't really think they care who teaches them, do you? They're just going through the motions so they can get a diploma and then a job."

Hattie sounded almost bored, speaking slowly, almost drawling. It had not been enough for her to offend me in a memo. Now she was doing it face to face. In what I hoped was a calm voice, I said, "Well, what you say may be true for some students, I suppose. But Vinny did have his admirers." As soon as the words left my lips, I knew they were the wrong thing to say. But maybe not. After all, I was not there to defend Vinny. It was too late for that. I was there to see if Hattie would implicate herself.

"Yeah? And that's probably what did him in. That pathetic little pansy was just too cute for his own good. He strutted around this place like he was king of the hill. And his students, like I said, they'd do anything for a piece of paper. Listen Bel, just between you and me, if somebody hadn't killed him, he probably would have ended up fighting a bias suit that you wouldn't believe." When Hattie spoke, her eyes focused and her lips moved with purpose. But when she was silent, her blinking eyes and still mobile mouth animated her face and she looked, well, batty. This was something new. I wondered if she was on medication or feeling guilty.

I decided to try another tack. "You know, Hattie. there's one thing I've always admired about you. You're so direct. I mean, you hated Vinny when he was alive and now that he's dead, you don't pretend any different. A lot of people in your position would try to gloss over their true feelings. . . ." I watched as her eyes became fixed and her lips became relatively still as she prepared to talk.

" 'In my positon' . . . What's that supposed to mean, Bel?" I heard the chair creak as she swiveled a little in it. Hattie was a large woman.

"Well, you know. They haven't found out who murdered Vinny yet and everybody knows how much you despised him. . . . I assume the cops have questioned you. . . ." I hesitated.

A smile of pure triumph stilled her mouth until she said, "As a matter of fact, they have. They asked me about Vinny's relationships with his students. And boy did I give them an earful." The woman was gloating.

It would have been expected that the police would question Hattie about the students' relationships with Vinny. After all, she was the FSE Program counselor. I realized it was probably Hattie who had steered them to Henry Granger, although he would stand out in a crowd.

"Of course. That must have been very helpful. You really do have your finger on the pulse of the Program," I said, crossing the fingers of my right hand below the level of her desk in a childish response to the lie that had flown so easily out of my mouth. "I expect you gave them something to go on. . . ." I was hoping this would elicit a little bragging from Hattie, and, sure enough, it did.

"Well you know that big black ex-convict with the tattoos? I heard he had a big run-in with Little Lord Fauntleroy over a term paper or something." Hattie looked very pleased with herself.

"You mean Henry Granger?" I asked innocently.

"Whatever," Hattie answered. "And I heard the police are very grateful to me for that info." She was leaning back in her chair now. Her eyes were no longer blinking and her lips had finally come to rest in a smug smile.

At the sight of that smirk, I didn't care if Hattie was Lizzie Borden incarnate. I wanted to wipe it off her face and have the last word too, so I said sweetly, "Well, I need some info too, Hattie. Have you had a chance to talk with Eleanor Chambers? You know—the FSE student I mentioned in my memo? The one who's been absent so much?"

I could tell from the way her eyes began blinking and her lips resumed twitching that Hattie had not contacted Eleanor. God, Vinny had been so right. The woman was worse than useless. "Well, I really need to know what's going on with her. Her uncle contacted the dean for a progress report. Don't worry, I told him you were on the case."

Now I had Hattie's attention. "Her uncle? Who's her uncle?"

"Josh something or other. I can't remember exactly. You know how it is when the memory goes, right Hattie?" I winked at her broadly. "But anyway, the dean is all in a state. So try to get her in, won't you?" Josh was the mayor's first name. Politics was Hattie's game. She was reaching for her Roladex as I rose from my chair, called "Thanks so much Hattie" over my shoulder, and slammed the door to her office behind me.

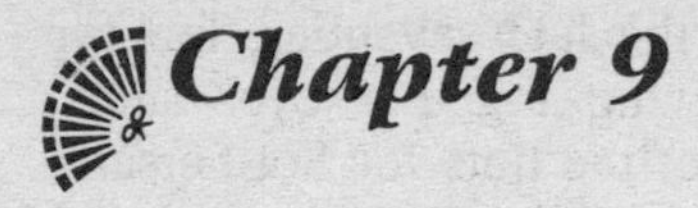

Chapter 9

Dear Professor Barrett,

Thank you for reaching out to me today. You are the only one who cares now. You are the only one who can touch me now. And you did touch me. Before I didn't realize that I meant anything to you.

Yours,
Eleanor

These words were scrawled on a piece of lined notebook paper wrapped around a one-pound bag of M&M's. A rubber band secured the paper around the all too familiar lumpy sack. The frozen elastic had snapped when I picked up the odd package, where it lay like an offering on the packed snow covering my doorstep. I had almost tripped over it. Rushing to make the meeting of the Citizens Committee to Preserve the Waterfront, I scanned the note and quickly stuffed it and the bag of goodies into my purse.

"So where's Sol? Honest to God, Bel, you two are living proof that environmental activism can be an aphrodisiac!" This was Marlene Proletariat's standard greeting. Longtime president of Hoboken's CCPW, Marlene has never gotten over the fact that Sol and I met at a CCPW party in the late seventies, left for coffee, and have been living together ever since. Sometimes I think she's got the hots for Sol herself.

"Hi Marlene. Sol's away again. But I'm here," I countered, wanting her to appreciate the sacrifice it had been to leave the warm sanctuary of home, where I should have been packing for my visit to my parents the next day. Going to graduate school had forced me to cut down on the amount of time I could give to the CCPW, but Sol was still a flaming activist.

And believe me, Hoboken, New Jersey, has been an activist's paradise since the latest revival of the Big Apple's economy once again upped the ante on real estate in the "other" river city. On every corner, developers slaver at the prospect of fringing our mile-square, low-rise town with high-rise hotels, offices, and luxury apartments. And at city hall, local officials slaver at the prospect of enough development-related pork to fatten on for the foreseeable future. The CCPW fights these forces of evil by crusading for adherence to zoning regs and for citizens' involvement in planning. In fact, tonight's meeting about rerouting the Bergen-Hudson Light Rail from the waterfront to the west side of town would never have come about without lobbying in the press by CCPW.

Actually, I was excited about the light rail. But hell, I'd be for hot-air balloons if I thought they'd reduce local traffic. And the Bergen-Hudson Light Rail, which will someday connect Bayonne with Fort Lee, is going to do just that. Like Sol and Marlene, I thought the new electric train should traverse Hoboken along the west side, providing an economic boost to an area still open to light industry and housing. The LR was, of course, being routed along the overly developed east side—you guessed it—on the waterfront.

As I shed my parka and settled into a chair near the front of the crowded room, I read the agenda handed to me by a young volunteer. Apparently this meeting was really a strategy session featuring speakers from historic Paulus Hook, Vinny's neighborhood in Jersey City. Some residents there had staged a letter-writing campaign in the press to protest routing the light rail along Essex Street, a quiet residential block in their neighborhood. Others had written in favor of the Essex Street route. Many voices had been heard. Marlene hoped we would stage a similar campaign. Copies of these letters, both pro and con, were distributed, and I took some for Sol.

Waiting for the meeting to start, I began reading through the letters. One of them struck a familiar chord. Perhaps I had come across it in the paper. Soon Marlene was introducing the first speaker, and, predictably, lulled by his earnest drone and the warm room, I began to nod. It had been a long day.

Ever since college, I've known only one surefire way to fight drowsiness. Reaching into my purse, I fumbled atavistically for the bag of M&M's. Before stuffing a fistful into my mouth, I dutifully offered some to the woman on my left, a dainty creature who looked at the large bag as if it held live snakes and declined. So much for my obligation to share.

My predilection for the little multicolored disks was well known among students and friends, so it hadn't really surprised me to find the bag of M&M's at my door. In fact, several neighbors regularly made a point of giving me their extra Halloween candy so they wouldn't eat it all themselves. I made a pretense of bringing it to work to share, but we all knew better.

Energized by the familiar rush of chocolate—the "Vitamin Ch" of fifty-something cognoscenti—surging through my body, I pulled out the note that had been wrapped around the bag and smoothed it out.

Just as I began rereading it, I heard a familiar stammer. When I recognized the voice of Arthur Hoffman, I couldn't believe my ears. Looking up quickly, I discovered I was right. There was Arthur Hoffman, big as life, addressing the crowd. I nearly fell off my chair.

"Wh . . . Wh . . . What they are doing, runnin' that train down Essex Street is wrong. I . . . I . . . It's gonna be right in people's livin' rooms." At this point Arthur gestured behind him to a map of Essex Street detailing every building in blue ink and outlining the proposed tracks in red. "It's gonna make noise. Every ten minutes a train will go by." Arthur glanced furtively at a piece of paper he held in one hand and hurried on. "M . . . M . . . More during rush hours. E . . . E . . . Every four minutes. Would you like a train in your livin' room every four minutes? W . . . w . . . would you?"

Now I didn't need M&M's to keep me awake. I was bursting with pride. Or, as Rebecca would say, I was "psyched." The fact that Arthur was here, speaking in public, made him one of my real success stories. I remember Arthur standing in my office, all six feet of him. A pale, lumbering eighteen-year-old, he weighed in at over two hundred pounds. Although his bulk threatened to overflow the office, Arthur was not big like a football player. Like me, he had more flab than fiber.

I had persuaded him to sit in Wendy's chair. "I . . . I . . . I . . ." Tears had welled up, spilling onto the collar of his blue plaid flannel shirt that was, I remember, buttoned all the way up to the top and at the ends of both sleeves, encasing his arms, which dangled like blue plaid sausages. He flushed, brandishing the Speech syllabus in one hand and clutching at the Kleenex I proffered with the other. "I . . . I . . . I . . . I can't talk in front of the class." When he finally got those words out, I allowed myself to exhale. Without realizing it, I had been holding my breath, praying that Arthur would be able to utter something about why he had followed me to my office after our first class meeting.

I placed a hand on each of his shoulders and looked him in the eye. Speaking softly, I said, "You may not want to talk in front of the class yet, but you can talk in front of me, and that's a start. Lots of students don't have the courage to approach a professor they don't know on the first day of class and express their concerns. And you did that. Bravo! I can tell you have what it takes. You'll be able to talk to God himself before the end of the semester." I maintained eye contact for a second or two after I had stopped talking.

Speech phobia is so common that I've had to develop a whole battery of approaches to enable students to transcend their terror. Sometimes I feel like a hypnotist or a coach or even a magician rather than just an English professor. You'd better believe I struggled long and hard with Arthur that semester, helping him select appropriate topics and develop outlines and listening to him rehearse.

It worked though. Arthur delivered all four required speeches to his classmates. He had no shortage of topics, because he had his heart set on being a fireman and was always studying for the qualifying test. I remember one speech on Hoboken landlords who set fire to their buildings to drive out renters and convert the buildings to condos. The speech itself wasn't great, but Arthur had illustrated it with a series of complex, meticulously drawn diagrams that had impressed us all. He had passed the course with a C.

And just look at him now! Why, he was voluntarily delivering a persuasive talk in front of an audience of strangers, fulfilling his obligation as a citizen in a participatory democracy. I stopped mentally patting myself on the back only when I realized that I was actually quoting from my own Speech syllabus.

After Arthur finished speaking, I applauded so hard that the woman sitting next to me who had refused the M&M's began to clap too. Several people spoke after Arthur, but I didn't hear them because I had moved to the back of the room for a reunion with my prize student. "I'm so proud of you, Arthur. You're really using your public speaking skills, aren't you? I had no idea you were concerned about the light rail." I accompanied my words with a bear hug, which Arthur clumsily returned. I rushed on: "I didn't know you were in Funeral Service Education until I saw you at Professor Vallone's funeral. What made you change your mind about being a fireman? How close are you to graduation?"

"Y . . . Y . . . Y . . . You don't know? I work in the RECC copy shop now." I seldom visited the dreary basement room that housed RECC's copy shop, preferring to rely on the campus mail system to pick up orders and deliver finished copy jobs. Arthur paused for a moment and then added, "I . . . I . . . I . . . I'm not thinking about the fire department no more. I . . . I . . . I . . . I didn't do so good on the test. I won't be graduating for a while. They got that algebra requirement now." He looked down a moment and then, with a touch of defiance that was new, he pronounced: "B . . . b . . . b . . . but it don't really matter about graduation. I like my job. It's a good, clean job. I . . . I . . . I . . . I like workin' around all them machines and copyin' stuff for the professors." Arthur had probably already dropped out, a casualty of the state's requirement that all students pass a proficiency test in algebra.

A model of politeness, he shifted the focus of the conversation. "H . . . h . . . h . . . how you doin', Professor Barrett? You know, I really miss your class and talkin' to you. Y . . . Y . . . You let me know when you want something copied, okay?"

Even if Arthur never graduated, he was living proof that even a little higher education was better than none, and that graduation rates are not the only way to measure the impact of the community college experience. I was just so pleased that RECC had helped transform Arthur from a sniveling, tongue-tied teen into this relatively poised and empowered young adult.

Let's face it. I was pleased with myself. More than pleased. I felt like the goddamn princess in the fairy tale whose kiss had worked wonders on the frog. Vanity, thy name is Professor. Walking home after the meeting, I floated just above the nearly deserted streets on a cloud of self-satisfaction. I had reached the doorstep of my house before I even remembered Eleanor's note.

Chapter 10

Dear Professor Barrett,

I can't take much more. I need to talk to you before I decide what to do next. And please don't tell me to see a counselor. Should I come during your regular office hours this week or some other time?

Very truly yours,
Gilberto Hernandez

Gilberto's note was attached to the outline of his research paper. I had planned to read some of those after the CCPW meeting. But as soon as I got home I checked my phone messages. My plans fell apart when I recognized Keith's voice. "Bel, I'm sorry, but I thought I should let you know. Rebecca got swiped by a car while she was riding her bike. She's having surgery at the U Medical Center to set the fractures. I have to go now. I want to be there when they take her up. I'll get back to you."

I never even took off my parka. I called a cab and threw some underwear and a clean pair of jeans in a backpack. During the fifteen-minute cab ride to Newark airport, I used my handy-dandy cell phone to leave messages for my department chair, my cat-sitting neighbor, and Betty and Illuminada.

I debated calling Sol. But what could he do from goddamn Prague? I decided not to call him until I had more information. Of course, calling Sadie and Ike was unthinkable. So for a brief moment I thought about it. I ached for a long-gone time when a call to my parents would have brought instant support and love. Now they needed those responses from me. I felt like curling up in the back seat of the cab, putting my thumb in my mouth, and wailing.

I was too worried to sleep, so I read student papers all the way to Chicago. That's when I happened upon Gilberto's note. I didn't like the sound of it. I recalled his black eye. Who had done that? Was it a fight over a girl? Or something more complicated, perhaps? Something to do with Vallone and Sons? I'd talk to him as soon as I got back. He wouldn't drop out of school before then. I scrawled "Call Gilberto Hernandez" on a Post-it.

It was dawn when, thanks to a lucky break with a connecting flight in Chicago, I finally landed in Seattle. By eight I was at Rebecca's bedside.

The scene that greeted me was every mother's nightmare. My daughter was swathed in bandages, apparently unconscious, and had two black eyes. A tube hooked up to her arm and a hanging plastic bag of clear fluid completed the diorama. For the first time since I had heard Keith's message, I felt faint.

A chair slid under me and I heard Keith's voice again, saying, "You don't look so good, Bel. Sit down. Rebecca's gonna be fine. Here." He handed me a Kleenex. "She'll have to wear that cast on her arm for a while, and her nose is a little out of joint." He smiled modestly at his joke. "And she's kinda bruised, but she's gonna be fine. I just talked to the doctor. Man, she's only been down from the recovery room a few hours." Suddenly Keith frowned. "She told me not to call you. She didn't want you to worry. But I figured you should know, so I called you anyway. I didn't expect that you'd come out here like this though." Keith's dimples, shadowed with stubble, were barely visible when he suddenly grinned. "Shit man, she'll be so glad to see you, I hope she'll forgive me."

"I'm glad you called me. And I'm so relieved. Of course she'll forgive you. You did the right thing. I am her mother, after all." I patted Keith's arm. This conversation triggered something struggling to surface in my muddled mind, but I couldn't spare the effort to prod it to consciousness. In time, it would float up and surprise me with its brilliance, I reassured myself. I was much more interested in Keith's next words.

"Listen, I'm gonna go downstairs and try to snag some breakfast and a few posies for her for when she really wakes up. Why don't I get you something too? You look like you could use it." What a thoughtful young man. And great dimples. No wonder my daughter had left the comforts of hearth and Hoboken to go camping out west with him. That had been several years ago now.

When Rebecca's eyelids finally fluttered open and lighted on me, I was rewarded for my sleepless night with a smile. I had barely smoothed her hair back from her face before she was asleep again.

That afternoon, after leaving the hospital, Keith and

I had an early dinner in a Mexican restaurant on Capitol Hill. Keith needed to describe in minute detail the sound of the car hitting Rebecca's bike wheel and the tangle of limbs, bike, and tree branches he had found when he reached her side. Listening to him, it occurred to me that I had been worrying about something happening to Mark in Israel, when it was Rebecca who had really been in danger in Seattle. She was at risk in a place where overcaffeinated, nature-loving, fitness freaks routinely run, bike, and hike in the damn rain up and down the damn mountains. Sighing, I raised my Corona in a private toast to bike helmets.

The beer-before-bed routine has not been practical for years, so I was not surprised when my bursting bladder awakened me in the middle of the night. After my late bathroom run, I stretched out on Keith's spare futon once again. Then suddenly I thought of what I'd been trying to remember all day and found myself sitting bolt upright. I was supposed to be in Charleston today or yesterday or whenever the hell it was back East! Oh my God! Sadie and Ike had been expecting me. They were still expecting me. They must have tried to call me. My God! How could I have forgotten about my visit to my parents? Surely a lapse of this magnitude could only be a sign of early onset Alzheimer's. Oh my God! My finger was wavering as I pushed the twenty or so buttons of my phone number and credit card and then listened to my messages.

"I'm glad you found the M&M's. Don't worry, I would never leave anything like that at school. You're right. We should talk. Call me at two–oh–one, five–five–five, nine–three–three–eight when you get home tonight."

Jesus. It was Eleanor Chambers. Even in my distracted state, I noted that Eleanor was chattier on my answering machine than she had been in person. I did not erase her message.

"Sibyl. This is your mother." I smiled reflexively. Like really Ma, no one else has called me Sibyl since first grade. Like I wouldn't recognize that raspy, Ethel-Merman-meets-Joan-Rivers voice. "I don't know where you are, so I pray nothing's happened to you. Maybe we got it wrong, the date you were coming. I don't like saying this to a machine. You shouldn't have to hear it on a machine either. I was waiting until you got here to tell you, but your father, Ike . . . his heart. Yesterday. Maybe you should give me a call."

"Maybe I should give *her* a call—not *us*?" I couldn't take in what I had heard. It was as unreal as sitting in Rebecca and Keith's apartment in the middle of Seattle in the middle of the night suddenly seemed. My father? It couldn't be. Ma was the one with health problems. But Ibickf? No way. There was one more message, a pathetic P.S., bleated into the night.

"Sibyl. Where are you? Your father. He's gone. Where are you? And where's Lenny?"

My finger hit the familiar keys even though I knew it was after midnight in Charleston. "Ma?"

"Oh Sibyl, thank God. Where are you? Your father, he had a heart attack. Did they tell you?" Her voice sounded a little fuzzy, subdued. Were they sedating her? And who the hell were "they" anyway?

"Yeah, Ma, I got your message. I love you." I mean what else was there to say? My parents had been married for more than sixty years. "I'm leaving for Charleston right away. I should be there by morning. Who's with you now?"

"I love you too. With me is the couple from next

door, the Biancos. They're Italian. He's a doctor. They keep comin' in and out. They're a very nice Italian couple." For Sadie, people had always come neatly labeled. "They heard me last night and called the ambulance. They came with us to the hospital. . . . But . . ." Her voice broke, and I heard a sob. "You and Lenny are coming, right?"

Oh boy. Mom had never accepted my decision to divorce Lenny, whom she described as "the best thing that ever happened to my *meshugana* daughter." She actually said "*meshugana*daughter" as if it were one word. And she'd never acknowledged Sol's role in my life even after he and I had been living together for several years. She treated Sol as if he were a total stranger who just happened to be sharing my house and my bed. Ma still lived for the day Lenny and I would reunite, presumably over the dead body of his second wife.

If I am the denial queen, then Sadie Bickoff is literally the mother of all denial queens. Had Ike's death pushed her over the thin line between denying reality and creating an alternate reality? Grief, fatigue, and worry made mush out of my mind. By the time I put down the receiver, I *felt* like a "*meshugana*daughter."

Especially without Ike. To him I'd been "Daddy's wondergirl." His unconditional love had been the bedrock upon which I had stood for my whole life. A word, a smile, or a hug from my father had sufficed to blunt the pain of maternal critiques, bad report cards, thoughtless boyfriends, and even the fallout from my decision to divorce Lenny. A world without my dad in it was unthinkable. I muffled my sobs in the pillow so as not to awaken Keith.

Before my late-morning flight to Charleston, I visited Rebecca. The doctor on rounds reassured me that

Rebecca would leave the hospital in a day or two. How would she manage? What about school? Work? She was a waitress—excuse me—a server. I hated that she lived so far away. I hated that I had to tell her about her grandfather too, but I had to. I cut to the chase. "You know, honey, I have to leave today. But I'm not going home." I read the puzzlement in her eyes. "Grandpa Ike died yesterday. He had a heart attack."

I reached for her hand and we hugged gingerly around the cast and bandages. "That really sucks, Mom," were Rebecca's very words, gurgled out as if they were bubbling up from under water. I hated seeing new pain line her brow and tears cloud her eyes.

"I couldn't have put it better myself," I acknowledged tearfully. "I never even worried about your grandfather. He was always in such good shape. Hardly ever even had a cold. He never had a problem with his heart." I pictured my dad dutifully pumping away on his excercise bike in his boxers every morning. I had to bite my lip and hold my breath to keep from adding my sobs to Rebecca's. When I could speak, I said, "Now Grandma needs me. I'll bring her back to Hoboken for a while." Should Rebecca be crying with her nose all bandaged?

"Grandma Sadie must be a wreck. How will she manage without Grandpa? And what about Sol? What does he think?" And then Rebecca blurted out what we used to call the sixty-four-thousand-dollar question. "How will you and Grandma live together? You'll drive each other crazy. Especially with Grandpa Ike gone." New tears filled her eyes, and she sounded so distressed that I couldn't stand it. This was a level-five chicken soup moment if there ever was one, and the untouched pot of cold coffee on her tray didn't cut it.

I wished I could comfort her with a story the way I used to. I was surprised when, moving to the edge of the bed where her bruised legs nearly reached the floor, she took my hand and began to tell me a story. "Remember when Grandpa Ike used to take me and Mark to Chinatown for dim sum? He'd let us eat whatever we wanted. He always explained what everything in those little baskets was and he'd never make us finish the ones we thought were gross inside." She hesitated for a second, "Remember the tiny tea set he bought me there once?" Rebecca's recollection prompted others, and before our bittersweet bedside visit ended, I realized that we had begun sitting shiva for my father.

It was a good thing too, because I felt very pressured to do what had to be done in Charleston and get back to work. Taking an occasional sick day or personal day is one thing, but faculty who miss more than that really make it hard for students to take a course seriously. And what about Vinny's murder? I needed to talk with Eleanor and Gilberto as well as to try to learn something about Vinny's business dealings and family life. It wasn't fair to drag Betty and Illuminada into this mess and then leave town.

Besides, I knew that if I kept busy enough, I wouldn't have time to feel. To that end, I planned every minute of the days ahead. As soon as I got to Charleston, I would arrange for Ike's body to be shipped to Hoboken. Then I'd pack whatever my mother would need for a few months. Only after carefully printing my plans on a series of numbered Post-its could I doze off into a fitful sleep. In my dream, my ex-husband Lenny and Ma were sharing a bag of M&M's with Eleanor Chambers.

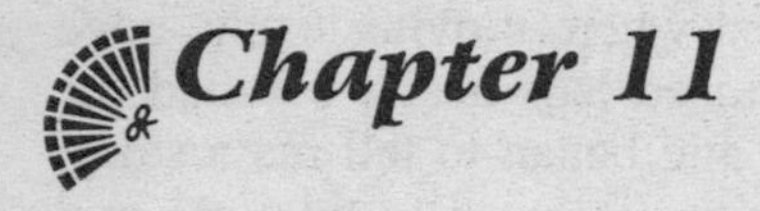

Chapter 11

To: Vaclav Grulich, Minister of the Interior
Czechoslovakia
Attention: Sol Hecht
Fax#011-42-02-21-944-321
Date: 03/03/96

Dear Sol,

I don't know if you got the phone messages I left at the hotel and at Vaclav's office, so I'm sending this to both places. Anyway, to repeat, my father died of a heart attack yesterday and I'm on my way to Charleston from Seattle (yes, you got that right), where I had to go on Thursday because Rebecca had been hospitalized after a biking accident. She's going to be fine. I'm okay, really. Don't even think about coming home for Ike's funeral. By the time you get this, it'll probably be over. We'll have a memorial service when Mark gets home and Rebecca can come and we can all be together. I'm really fine. Don't worry.

Love,
Bel

I tensed when I saw my mother's Valium-glazed eyes widen as she took in Betty's dark skin. "Mrs. Bickoff, how terrible to lose your husband. I'm so sorry." Betty enfolded my mother in a hug and then wrested Sadie's purse from her thin hand. She led the dazed and bedraggled figure hobbling within the cage of her walker toward the terminal exit, where Illuminada waited with the car. Then Betty ran back to help me with the rest of Ma's luggage.

Let's face it. Ma and I were a crisis waiting for management. The familiar take-charge gleam in Betty's eye was such a welcome sight to me that the sobs I'd been swallowing for days almost erupted at my first glimpse of her. Betty was primed for action. After a brief "So sorry about your Dad, Bel," Betty talked nonstop until we reached the car. "Illuminada convinced the cat-sitter to let us into your house, so we put some juice, eggs, yogurt, English muffins and other stuff in your fridge. And Illuminada's mom made some *ropa veija*. We put that in the freezer. And I had a brainstorm. You said on the phone you needed someone to stay with your mom while you teach? Well, I've got someone in mind. You know her. And she'll work for free."

As we entered the house, I impatiently kicked aside a small parcel with a salmon pink rose on it lying on the doorstep. Briefly I wondered if I should have brought my mother here within the orbit of the loopy Eleanor Chambers. It was too late to reconsider now, and besides, there was no choice. I was Sadie and Ike's only offspring. "You still have that damned cat. Emily Bronte, right?" Ma asked. We were home.

I settled Ma into Rebecca's old room, where my redecorating was limited to ripping down a frayed poster of Don Johnson and resolving to get some fresh flowers. "Your father was a good man—my best friend. And what a father. You were the apple of his eye. Right from day one. Right, Ike? You always used to call her the light of your life. And you too, Lenny. Ike's always loved you like a son. Right, Ike?"

Ma's words, shifting as they did from reality to fantasy, raised goose bumps on my arms as I filled the dresser drawers with scarves, purses, and lingerie. "See, Ma, your underwear? In the top drawer. And sweaters in the next one." I focused on arranging Ma's familiar knit outfits in Rebecca's closet.

Sadie had eaten lightly, showered with my help, and was dozing fitfully in bed by the time Betty and Illuminada returned with Boston Chicken and Ben & Jerry's Chocolate Chip Cookie Dough ice cream. I was so tired I could hardly stagger to the door to let them in. But the sight of my two friends and all that forbidden food energized me.

"I really don't know how to thank you guys. I couldn't have managed today without your help."

Illuminada's cerise fingernails were flashing as she opened the bags of food. "Right Bel, without us you're an incapable cream puff, we know that. *Dios mio*, let's get on with it. We're not finished helping you yet."

"Yeah," Betty said through a mouthful of mashed potatoes. "Check this out, girlfriend. It's so amazing. Remember Pearl Hoskins? Henry Granger's grandmother? The LPN?"

I actually stopped chewing for a minute. I had to smile at how pleased with themselves they were. "Yes. But I don't really know her. And besides, Ma doesn't really need an LPN. She's going to be fine. She's a really tough cookie. And her walking, it's just arthritis. I mean maybe there's something . . ."

Betty and Illuminada exchanged a swift glance before Illuminada spoke. "I know your mom's not herself now. Actually, I think she's doing really well, considering. My mom was a lot younger when my dad died. *Caramba*, she was clinically depressed for almost a year." Illuminada was shaking her head and staring at a chicken leg.

Her next words were more animated. "Besides, Bel, what about you? You have to be able to go to class without worrying yourself to death about what's going on here." Illuminada looked around quickly and continued, "And *chiquita*, believe me, you don't want to go into debt to come up with five or six hundred bucks a week to pay a caregiver either. And what if she doesn't show up or doesn't treat your mom right?" Now she was pointing the chicken leg at me to underscore her words.

That's true. I'm the only one I allow to be mean to my mom, I thought, remembering how in the last two days I'd arranged for the shipment of Ike's body, gotten a refill of Ma's Valium, packed up the dazed widow, and hustled her out of Charleston. Aloud I said, "Well, I certainly can't afford to hire somebody to stay here with her for long. I'm going to have to get Ma set up with a doctor first and then, later on . . ."

"Later on is later on. Right now, Pearl Hoskins is willing to work for nothing. Well, not really nothing. She wants to make it easier for you to get back to helping Henry. That's her motive. Think of it as an in-kind deal." Betty paused to pull a corn muffin apart with her fingers. "And besides, she's competent and decent too. And Illuminada has already checked her references and her licensing. At least you should talk to her. She's coming at ten tomorrow to interview." Betty was adamant.

"We've got a few other things to lay on you, but they can wait. You look so beat. Besides, I don't like talking to you when you're sober." Illuminada's serious expression belied her attempt at levity. She went on. "I found this outside. Do you have a clue as to what it means?" She held up the small package of M&M's with a now rather wilted-looking frozen rose tied to it with a frozen white bow. The crumpled note under the ribbon read, "Be my Valentine. Eleanor."

"Yeah, I know what it means," I said wearily. "It means Eleanor Chambers has misunderstood my behavior. She thinks I'm interested in her romantically, just like she thought Vinny was. She's sending me notes and leaving messages on my machine. And now that I'm back, she'll probably start following me around. Christ, she may be out there right this minute, for all I know." I began to gouge the bottom of the ice cream container with my spoon.

Illuminada's brow contracted. "I thought you asked Batty Hattie to talk to Eleanor about her absences. She *is* Eleanor's counselor, after all. Did she make contact?"

"Hattie called me to say that she phoned Eleanor at home and at work and sent her a letter asking her to come in, but Eleanor hasn't responded. That's really all Hattie can do. Tell me again, what time is Pearl Hoskins coming?" I asked through a yawn.

"Ten sharp. Get some sleep. And remember, Eleanor's no problem until you reject her. Just don't do that, okay Bel?" Illuminada was using her serious voice, the voice she used to advise victims of spousal abuse how to get restraining orders. Then she changed persona to add, "Besides, you two make a cute couple." She moved quickly so as to dodge the napkin I lobbed at her.

"*Dios mio!* It's late. Betty, when is Victor coming to pick you up?"

"Victor?" I repeated numbly. "Victor who? Who the hell is Victor?" Betty's sudden smile transformed her face. "Victor Vallone. Hey girl, think you're the only one who can play detective or, for that matter, get a Valentine card?"

"The ice maiden's in love," said Illuminada.

Betty had not allowed a man within spitting distance of her since her husband had walked out over ten years ago. Whenever I asked her about her self-imposed celibacy, she'd say, "Been there. Done that. Don't need to mess with it again." She maintained a civil relationship with her ex-husband, Randy's father, and she claimed no need for another partner.

"Betty, tell me what's going on." I was giving orders now. "I leave town for a few days and while I'm gone your inner nun vanishes and you're making it with a white undertaker? Is that what I'm hearing?" I was wide awake now.

"Betty, if you don't tell her, I'm going to tell her for you," threatened Illuminada, impatient as always with our word games.

"Okay, okay." Betty's smile contrasted sharply with her words, which referred back to poor Vinny's murder. "Bel girl, I'm sorry, but I don't buy your theory about the Chambers woman. I mean, she's a possibility for sure, but I figured we better look at the other possibilities too." Betty was in her element now. Her eyes glittered and her diction was crisp.

"Vinny was in business with his brother, and their mother died recently, right? Business partners get greedy and so do brothers. I figured maybe there was something going on at the funeral home, or a fight over their mother's will. Who knows? Also, I figured, in the business there could be an employee with a grudge."

As always, I was impressed by Betty's clearheaded, methodical thinking. None of this intuition stuff for her. Nevertheless, I couldn't resist teasng her a lttle. "Honestly Betty, couldn't you just put an ad in *New York* magazine like everybody else if you wanted to meet somebody? Did you have to make up these elaborate pretenses?"

Now Illuminada was grinning. "People who sit through long, boring meetings about zoning laws and parking in order to meet men shouldn't talk." To acknowledge her snide reference to how I'd met Sol, I thumbed my nose at her.

Ignoring both of us, Betty went on. "So I talked President Woodman into inviting Vic Vallone to serve on the RECC Development Fund Board and then made an appointment for Woodman to extend the invite personally. But I made the appointment on a day when I knew Woodman would be out of town, and then I let him persuade me to go in his place." Betty raised two thumbs in a gesture of self-congratulation.

"Vic and I met and we talked. And then we talked some more and it was getting late, and he asked me to have dinner with him. So I did." And then my tough-talking, hard-nosed friend giggled. "He's pretty cool for a white dude." Betty's smile was now beatific.

"Yeah. He's okay, if you like undertakers, I guess." Illuminada couldn't resist another little dig.

Just as I was opening my mouth to speak, Betty continued. "And before you even ask about him being white"—she paused dramatically—"let me remind you, some of my best friends are white." We all groaned.

"But listen up. There's more. Vic had been about to go to the police about another suspect when I talked with him," Betty announced. "I haven't even discussed this with Illuminada yet, so you're both out of the loop."

"Well, bring us in. I don't have all night. And Bel is a walking zombie." Maybe it was because she was used to being paid by the hour, but Illuminada was always watching the clock.

"Okay. There's an employee at the funeral parlor, an intern at RECC in fact. His name is Gilberto Hernandez. Do you teach him?" Betty was looking at me.

"Uh-huh, I do. He's a quiet young man. A fairly good student. He's almost ready to graduate. Very handsome and *very* intense." I recalled Gilberto's black eye and his note. "But what motive would Gilberto have had? Almost all the students really liked Vinny." As I uttered these words, the image of the irate Henry Granger denouncing Vinny as a "fat-ass white faggot" blazed through my brain. "Unless maybe there was a problem between them at the funeral parlor . . ."

Betty continued, speaking seriously, obviously eager to share her new man's suspicions. "Vic says Gilberto and Vinny were lovers, but they had a big fight." When nobody said anything, Betty looked at me and said, "I thought you'd talk with the kid, Bel, sound him out, see what you think. And," she added now with a look at Illuminada, "I was hoping that you'd check him out too, you know, does he have a record and everything."

"Yes. That's easy. He's overdue for a conference

anyway. I can talk to him," I assured her.

Illuminada nodded and stood up abruptly. Looking at Betty she said, "I'm beat. If Romeo's not coming to get you, Juliet, I'll drive you home."

Chapter 12

To: Bbarrett@circle.com
From: Caregiverssupportgroup@SOS.com
Subject: Delusions, depression, denial
Date: 03/07/98 04:30:15

Bel honey,

Just got your SOS. You got a load on your shoulders that would weigh down a mule. You say your recently widowed 82-year-old mama talks to her late husband and your ex-husband and ignores your efforts to reason with her. The bad news is it sounds like she's pretty disoriented and confused. Shock and grief can do that to people, specially older folks. I suggest you get her to a shrink ASAP. The good news is you don't have to wear yourself out reasoning with her. She won't listen.

You say you've lost your privacy because your mama talks to you while you're in the shower and on the phone and even comes into your room to talk before you're out of bed in the morning. Well, you're right. You have lost your privacy. The good news here is your mom's talking to you and not to somebody dead or gone. Seriously, we got to learn to count our blessings.

And Bel honey, maybe you could talk to the shrink awhile yourself and tell him all about the roses and the M&M's and the body in the river.

A menopause support group had sustained me through hot flashes, insomnia, and vaginal dryness, so I didn't see why a caregivers' support group couldn't give me a few tips on how to survive life with Mother. Shortly after Sadie moved in, I e-mailed the caregivers' support group. It had been a really bad day.

First of all, Ma came into the bathroom during my shower, stood leaning on her walker outside the shower curtain, and said brightly, "Sibyl, your father doesn't care for the television reception here. He asked me if you and Lenny were planning to get cable. Are you?" Great. While I tried to dream up an appropriate and civil reply, I realized that my estrogen patch was no longer on my butt where it belonged. This was a first, and I panicked. *How long had it been missing? Minutes? Days? Had I already begun to shrivel into a human prune from estrogen deprivation?* Ma was still chattering away while I dropped to my knees and began to crawl around the tub groping for the missing magic disc. It was a little like looking for a lost contact lens in a rainstorm at the bottom of the Grand Canyon. The patch wasn't there. Even after I had replaced it with a new one, I felt uneasy, wondering what the effect of the missing elixir would be and expecting to be plunged back into the land of the perpetually perspiring at any moment.

As if that weren't enough, it had snowed again during the night. Resigned, I suited up and went out to shovel before leaving for work. But when I got outside, I saw that the sidewalk in front of the house, the path to the stoop, and the stoop steps had already been cleared of snow. At first I thought my neighbor had done it to repay me for watering his plants while he was away over Christmas. Then I spotted the single yellow rose sticking out of the blue plastic bag encasing the *New York Times*. My stomach knotted. I knew who had shoveled. I allowed myself a quick glance down the snowy street. There was no sign of Eleanor. Relieved, I hastily withdrew into the warm house.

But I couldn't stay there for long, because it was the day of our class trip. One of the first things I had done when I returned to work was arrange for my Funeral Service Education students to visit the Egyptian exhibits at the Metropolitan Museum of Art. The snow would be a nuisance, but it wouldn't deter us from our pilgrimage. We would travel from Jersey City to New York on the PATH train and then take another subway uptown.

Normally I'd be as excited about this adventure as the students were, but I was tired, sad, and not a little frazzled. I needed to shepherd thirty people through the New York City subway system to ogle a bunch of long-dead Egyptians like I needed another five pounds around my middle. But a promise is a promise. And Wayne Simpson, the adjunct who had been hired to replace Vinny, had agreed to go along with us. Wayne seemed pleasant enough and knowledgeable, but not very dynamic. I didn't envy him. Vinny was a tough act to follow.

Gilberto and I had agreed to talk on the subway, so I wasn't surprised when he settled into the empty seat next to me as the train pulled out of the station. He seemed smaller than I remembered him. The skin around his previously black eye had yellowed and his handsome face was wan and pinched. Now instead of looking like a male model, he more closely resembled a poster child for CARE.

"Sorry about your dad, Professor Barrett," he mumbled.

"Thank you, Gilberto," I replied. "What was it you wanted to see me about?" I tried to keep my voice low key.

"It's kinda personal," the young man answered, looking around the subway car where his classmates chattered and struck postures for Alan, who had brought a camcorder.

"Nobody's paying any attention to us, Gilberto. They're all posing for Alan," I said reassuringly. "What's on your mind?"

"I just want some advice," he said, lowering his voice so I had to lean over to make out his next words, "before I go to the cops."

"To the police? You've lost me. Wait. Does this have anything to do with your black eye?" I kept my voice low too.

Gilberto grimaced. "No way. Not exactly. Well sorta. It has to do with Vinny." His use of Vinny's first name instead of "Professor Vallone" jarred me. Gilberto must have sensed my reaction, for he added quickly, "I guess he never said nothin' about it, but me and him were close—very close." Vic Vallone was right. Gilberto and Vinny had been lovers.

"No, he didn't." Everybody within shouting distance knew I thought profs who had sex with their students were unethical slimeballs, so Vinny certainly wouldn't have told me that he and Gilberto were a couple. I wondered what else Vinny hadn't told me. Henry Granger had been right about Vinny. The man *had* had secrets. To Gilberto I said simply, "Then you've lost a lot more than a teacher. I'm so sorry," and I meant it. I resisted the urge to pat Gilberto's shoulder. Instead I asked, "But what advice is it that you want? What were you thinking of going to the police about?" I was prodding now, aware that we had already passed Exchange Place and our ride would end in a few more stops.

"Maybe it's nothing, but it's driving me crazy, man. I don't know what to do." I waited patiently while Gilberto tugged on a strand of his wavy black hair and then continued. When he spoke again, his voice was muffled and his breathing irregular. I thought maybe he was trying to keep from sobbing. "A week before Vinny was murdered, him and his brother had a big fight. I was workin' in the prep room and they were in the office. Teresa, she's the receptionist, had already left for the day. I heard them yellin', so I went up to see what was goin' on." Gilberto shook his head as if to ward off a painful memory. Then he added, "I was embarrassed to go in 'cause, man, Victor was really goin' off on Vinny. I just stood outside the door to make sure he was okay. Then I went back downstairs."

"What were they arguing about?" Betty hadn't mentioned anything about an argument between the brothers.

Gilberto sighed and said wearily, "It was something about money from their mother and something else about the business. . . . Victor was real mad. Professor Barrett, I keep thinkin' I should go to the cops. Do you think I should?"

Just then Alan Wiener zoomed in on us, camcorder in hand. "Smile, Professor B. Hernandez, you too." He moved away just as we reached our stop.

"Gilberto, let me think about this. I'd like to talk to you more about it, okay?" Gilberto nodded as we stood and joined the other passengers exiting the train.

"Man! Look at this place! Could you all line up on these steps, so I can shoot everybody walking in?" Obediently we formed a row so Alan could document our arrival at the Met.

I noticed Henry Granger looking around the Great Hall in silence, his eyes barely blinking as he took in the marble floors, the domed ceilings, the larger than life bouquet of winter blooms at the information desk and the massive columns. I also watched him size up the two security guards at the entrance. "Pretty spectacular, isn't it, Henry?" I said before rushing off to make a donation and get buttons for everybody. "Would you please get everyone a floor plan from the information desk?"

When I returned, my students were all studying floor plans. "Look! They got African art here too. Can we go see that? I mean after the mummies?" Joevelyn sounded like a kid. The Met was working its predictable magic, and I felt my spirits lift a little for the first time in weeks as I shepherded my charges a few steps to the right, straight into the heart of ancient Egypt.

For the next two hours, both Wayne and I worked hard, so hard that I actually forgot about Rebecca's broken arm, Middle Eastern suicide bombers, Vinny's murder, and my poor mother's delusional *meshugass*. I existed in a space above even the agony I felt anew whenever I recalled my father. Teaching is like making love. If you're doing it right, you have no thought for anything else. I'd taught my way through two uncomfortable pregnancies, a hideous divorce, Rebecca's high-school romance with a thirty-five-year-old psychopath, and Mark's bloody fling with urban skateboarding, so I knew how to escape into my work.

"Professor, what's a 'minor wife'?" asked Adamo, genuine puzzlement in his voice.

"Satrapy? What kinda trap is that?" from a mystifed Joevelyn.

Even Alan was stumped by "schismatic monophysite doctrine." I overheard him muttering, "Who writes this stuff anyway—professors?"

Wayne and I had tried to prepare them for what they would see by reviewing Egyptian religious beliefs and funerary customs, but the scope of the exhibit, which spans the centuries between paleolithic grave goods and Islamic jewelry, threatened their sense of mastery. It was important to help them connect what they were seeing with their own experience and knowledge.

Predictably, the mummies saved the day. I overheard Henry saying caustically to Adamo, "Yo man, check how they did this old lady. She was poor, so she didn't get no jewels or carving on her anthropoid coffin. And they just made it out of a log. What a dis. But this rich dude here, he got eyes made of jewels 'n'shit. See? Nothin's changed."

It was right about then that I noticed Gilberto had disappeared. When there was still no sign of him after a few minutes, I assumed he'd made a trip to the men's room. But I checked with my colleague Wayne anyway. "Wayne, have you seen Gilberto?"

"Yeah. He said to tell you he had business to take care of and took off." Was Gilberto going to the police? I had hoped to talk with him again and learn more about the argument he overheard between the Vallone brothers. And I hadn't even gotten him to talk about his own blowup with Vinny, which Victor had mentioned to Betty.

After that, I was really not in the mood to listen to Alan wax rhapsodic over the canopic vessels. "Man! Imagine this jug filled with intestines and this one with the liver. Isn't that awesome? And then they stuff the body cavity with something to fill it out, see?" The depraved young man was actually pulling on my sleeve as he pointed to a stunning alabaster jar with its human-headed stopper. I struggled to picture it filled with golden chrysanthemums instead of guts and gore.

We were really rushing by the time we got to the Sackler wing, home to the reconstructed Temple of Dendur. Entering, I blinked at the sudden infusion of light pouring in through the wall of slanted glass that forms one side of this miraculous showcase. Alan was inspired to begin shooting again as he approached the ancient funerary temple, which had been transported to New York and reassembled stone by stone.

"Yo! Professor! Ain't this graffiti here? Look!" It was Adamo beckoning me beyond the first archway and into the temple itself. I looked at the ancient stone wall originally commissioned by Augustus and covered with hieroglyphics and—would you believe—there is graffiti dating from the nineteenth century.

Adamo flashed a rare grin at his discovery, and I was about to launch into a discussion of the age-old need people have to leave their mark, when suddenly I felt the tiny hairs on my arms stiffen and my words catch in my throat. Through the arch of the temple I had glimpsed the familiar figure of a tall, white woman with nondescript brown hair move stealthily out of view just a few feet away. When I emerged from the temple, she was gone.

That fleeting and fragmentary sighting of Eleanor

and the revelations and disappearance of Gilberto troubled me. On the subway home, Alan's earnest question about how the Egyptian embalmers managed to pull a corpse's brains out through his or her nose with a hook failed to elicit more than a groan from me.

By the time I had finished teaching my afternoon class and arrived home, I barely had the energy to log on to the *Jerusalem Post*. Things were relatively quiet in Israel. God was fulfilling his part of the bargain. I better get busy on mine.

Pearl was waiting for Henry to pick her up, so we all shared some of the tepid wonton soup and eggplant with garlic sauce I had brought in. It hadn't taken me long to become completely dependent on Pearl's common sense and reassuring presence. She and Ma were getting along remarkably well. Pearl treated Ma with respect and affection, and Ma didn't seem to be driving Pearl crazy at all. I even overheard them chuckling together once or twice when I arrived home. I guess other people's mothers are like other people's kids, charming and polite. They only let their inner pain-in-the-ass personae out with those who offer unconditional love.

"You look a little drawn this afternoon, Pearl. Ma giving you a hard time?" I remarked as I noticed that the tiny lines that feathered out from the corners of Pearl's eyes seemed deeper than usual and her shoulders sagged a little as she ate.

"No, your mother's an angel," said Pearl, evidencing a heretofore unrecognized gift for hyberbole. I noticed Ma lean over and pat Pearl's hand.

"Pearl's worried about her grandson," Ma interjected. Ma has never been known for her reluctance to speak for others. "She doesn't like the people he's been seeing. You remember the summer you dated that bearded beatnik character who wrote those disgusting poems and read them in coffeehouses in Greenwich Village? You were always coming home at all hours. Your father and I were very upset, weren't we, Ike? It's hard when kids don't know how to choose their friends."

In spite of the frisson of fear I felt every time Ma addressed Ike or Lenny, I had to smile. She was talking about Hal Klinger. The summer before I left for Vassar had been a magical few months. Back then, Hal's rabble-numbing rants and lazy smile, Chet Baker's falsetto crooning, and a Chianti bottle with a candle in it had been my idea of high romance.

Pearl interrupted my flight down memory lane when she sighed and said, "Yeah. Henry's been hangin' out some with a friend from before. From before he went away, I mean. He say he tryin' to bring him to Christ. But he out late sometimes and he seem kinda, I don't know, kinda temper-mental, you could say."

Before I had a chance to digest this information, the doorbell chimed and Pearl stood up. "That's prob'ly him. Don't pay me no mind. It's prob'ly nothin'. Now you sleep good, you hear?" Pearl gave Ma a hug. To me she said, "Mrs. Bickoff's comin' along. She taught me to play gin today." Winking broadly, Pearl was putting her arm into the sleeve of her coat as she uttered her exit line. "Don't suppose the Lord or Pastor Johnson gonna mind a little gamblin' if it help my patient, right?"

Chapter 13

March 7, 1996

Dear Professor Barrett,

Please accept my condolences on the death of your father. How fortunate that your mother is able to be with you during this difficult time in her life. And I am glad too that your daughter is recovering from her accident.

That said, I want to dissuade you from "putting your graduate studies on hold" because of "unforseen professional and personal problems." The murder of the author of the teaching journals you were analyzing is, I agree, a setback. But Bel, you told me that you'd been waiting years to start doctoral work. I applaud you for beginning and remind you that for those of us who remember when Gloria Steinem was a Playboy bunny but forget the names of our students, procrastination is a zero sum strategy.

You have also spoken movingly of the obstacles your own students overcome to attend classes: They raise families, hold jobs, and still manage to study full-time. Would they let a few personal problems and a dead colleague stand between them and their goals? Not likely.

I look forward to seeing you in class next week. When you have time, we can reschedule our conference.

Sincerely,
Anita Holland, PhD

"Takes an old pro to appreciate another old pro," was my thought as I read Professor Holland's letter. I'd used similar tactics myself to persuade many students to stay in school. She was right. I was determined to reclaim my life.

Ironically, it was research that was going to help me do so. I still wanted to know everything there was to know about Eleanor Chambers. She couldn't be as nutty as she seemed and not have a history.

But the one I was really curious about now was Victor Vallone. I wanted to have a few words with that man myself. He had some explaining to do. Why hadn't he told Betty about his argument with Vinny? About their dispute over their mother's will? And what about those caskets? Frankly, it made me very nervous to think that one of my best friends was falling in love with a guy who might very well be a fratricidal madman. I had left a guarded message on Illuminada's machine. She was coming over after dinner. I had not invited Betty.

"Ma, don't you ever get sick of chicken breasts?" Ever since the early seventies when some health guru had first touted the virtues of the boneless and skinless chicken breast, Sadie Bickoff had prepared these boring poultry parts in every conceivable style and served them to Ike on the nights she was not plying him with broiled fish. My kids had grown up expecting their grandparents to sprout feathers and fins. And for what? My poor father had had a heart attack and died anyway. I hoped that in heaven he was eating lamb chops again.

Desperate to avoid broiling yet another bird boob, I had stopped off for a classic Hoboken treat—pizza from Benny Tudino's—and Ma and I had an early dinner. To my relief, she finished an entire slice. As she swallowed her last bite of that thin, crisp crust, I said, "Try some with the peppers and onions, Ma. It's still a little warm."

"Half. I can only eat half." She carefully bisected a wedge and transferred one of the resulting slivers onto her plate. Always thin, my mother now seemed skeletal, even wearing a bulky sweater and the beige knit pantsuit that screamed 1977.

"It was a nice funeral, don't you think?" Ma asked me for the hundredth time since the decidedly underwhelming private ceremony I'd orchestrated over a week ago. Our few and distant relatives and the even fewer surviving able-bodied friends of Sadie and Ike still in the area comprised a group of barely more than the ten Jewish adults required for a minyan. Betty and Illuminada, whom I'd told not to bother coming, had just looked at each other and elevated their eyebrows. Of course they had ignored me and sat together during the brief ceremony, a yarmulka bouncing precariously atop Betty's dreads. I did not shed a tear as Rabbi Gottesman wove the words I'd jotted down for her about my father into a eulogy. I thought of the funeral as a token experience, a holding maneuver until spring, when the kids and Sol could be around.

Since Ike had wanted to be cremated, we were

spared the perilous journey through the snowy burbs to the cemetary. After the service we made our way to my house for a kiddush *cum* lunch. That lox-and-bagel-filled hour and a half was the extent of our official mourning period. I could not miss another day of classes.

But that night, after I'd given Sadie her Valium and kissed her good night, my tears came. Alone in bed, I could no longer will out childhood memories. They filled my head and hurt my heart. Once again I heard Ike's voice saying, "Bel, your mother's tired. She doesn't mean to snap at you." Or with his arms circling me, "Bel, hold the bat like this and bend your knees. Atta girl!" Sleep eluded me for hours. When I did finally close my eyes, I dreamed that a burglar had broken into the house and stolen all my family photos. I was condemned to live surrounded by blank picture frames and albums filled with page after page of empty cellophane pockets.

Sadie was still focused on the rabbi's eulogy. "It was true what the rabbi said about your father, wasn't it? He was a devoted husband and father. Just like the rabbi said, he was ahead of his time the way he always helped with the housework and the way he took care of you. If I had a dollar for every diaper that you changed, I'd be a rich woman, wouldn't I, Ike?"

Ma's chats with Dad rendered me speechless with fear and embarrassment. I feared for her sanity, and I felt embarrassed to bear witness to her intimate and private conversation. She seemed to sense my discomfort and addressed me directly in an ordinary way: "So Sibyl, what are you doing tonight? More schoolwork? Every night it's papers, papers, papers. Or you sit at that computer like it was a crystal ball."

"You know I always have a lot of essays to read.

Besides, it's so nasty out that I'm glad to stay home where it's snug and warm." I wanted to keep the conversation going because Ma was making sense and maneuvering the other half slice of pizza onto her plate.

I was about to explain that Illuminada was stopping by when Ma said, "Lenny likes more nightlife. You know that. You kids should try to get out more. Your father and I don't mind. We'll watch a little TV and go to bed early."

Ma's appointment with the geriatric psychiatrist was the following week. I was counting the minutes.

By the time Illuminada rang the bell, I had settled Mom in her room with the TV on low and the new night-light glowing softly. When I leaned over to kiss her, I said, "Ma, call me if you need to get up. I don't want you to fall. Sleep well." She rewarded me with a smile and a surprisingly tight hug. Was that smile for me or at the prospect of a quiet night with Dad in front of the TV?

The cold air that blew into the house when I let Illuminada in actually felt good against my tear-stained cheeks. I stood in the doorway a few extra seconds, taking deep breaths and blowing my nose. After taking in my blotchy face and the wad of Kleenex in my hand, Illuminada remarked, "I never said it would be easy."

She ought to know. Illuminada's mother, Milagros Sanchez, had been living upstairs from the Guttierez family for many years. But Milagros was a plump, smiling woman who brewed coffee and made delicious flan. What could Illuminada know of living with Sadie Bickoff, who even on a good day had always measured her smiles and spelled *dessert* F–R–U–I–T?

"She is unreal," I replied. It's like she's not even

here sometimes. Hell, it's like I'm not even here. She talks to Lenny a lot. Right now she's watching TV with my father. Your mom is a piece of cake compared to mine." I was slightly embarrassed to hear the childish whine in my voice.

"*Caramba*, Bel, Milagros Santos is a religious fanatic who talks to God and at least three saints and has been known to see the Virgin Mary in the bottom of a juice glass as well as in the bathroom mirror. Now she's totally gone off because Luz finally has a boyriend, but the poor kid isn't Cuban. He's Filipino. So now my mother's not talking to my daughter, her only grandchild. Like I told you, it isn't easy." With a wry smile, Illuminada threw off her coat, peeled off her boots, and curled up on the loveseat.

"It sure as hell isn't. And you know what I think about now?" I didn't wait for an answer. "What we're going to be like when we get up there. You think our kids won't be complaining to their friends? I know for sure I won't be talking to saints or dead people. I'm going to be talking to myself. I already do. And I answer myself too. And you know what?" Again, my question was rhetorical. "It's very satisfying." Having made this confession, I curled up on the other end of the loveseat, leaving a spot for Virginia Woolf on the cushion between us.

"*Dios mio*, you're right. I already talk to myself in two languages." Illuminada flashed an impish grin that disappeared as suddenly as it had come. She looked grave when she said abruptly, "So what did you drag me over here for? And where's Juliet? Getting it on over dinner with the undertaker again?"

It did feel strange not to have Betty there. "I didn't tell her. I want to talk to you about her and Victor Vallone. I'm worried about Betty. She may actually be in danger." I reached for a pistachio nut from the bowl on the coffee table.

Illuminada sighed with familiar exasperation and, helping herself to a pistachio, said, "You have exactly one second to tell me what the hell you're talking about."

"Remember Gilberto Hernandez? My student who's an intern at Vallone and Sons? The one Victor said was Vinny's lover?" When Illuminada nodded, I went on, "Well, I talked briefly with Gilberto yesterday. He says they were lovers. But that's neither here nor there. Gilberto says that a week or so before Vinny's murder he overheard a loud argument between Victor and Vinny about the money from their mother's will and the business. Victor doesn't know Gilberto was eavesdropping. Gilberto thinks he should go to the cops." Then, as an afterthought, I said, "And last week Gilberto showed up in class with an enormous shiner."

By the time I paused, there was a small pile of pistachio shells on the coffee table next to Illuminada. "*Caramba*," she exclaimed. "Didn't he give any details of the argument?"

"No, although we did agree to talk again. I already have a conference scheduled with him tomorrow about his research paper." The pile of nutshells next to me was growing.

"You know, *chiquita*," said Illuminada thoughtfully, "I was afraid of this. Family members make such good suspects. That's why Betty went to see Victor in the first place, remember?" Illuminada's brow formed a sharp line over her eyes now as she reflected on the latest turn of events. "And then she came back all starry-eyed, like a goddamn teenager, Bel. You should have seen her. . . . I didn't have the heart to burst her bubble. But I should have said something right away." Illuminada slapped her leg in frustration. "*Dios mio*, she'll never listen to us now. She's really crazy about him."

"How the hell were you supposed to know the ice maiden would melt? I mean, don't beat yourself up over this. We just have to keep an eye on her, that's all." I didn't like to see Illuminada blame herself for not being omniscient. She was not the first to be surprised by where the flying fat baby aimed one of his arrows. And she was such a perfectionist that even the hint of a lapse or mistake on her part sent her into orgies of self-flagellation. I like to think I have outgrown that predilection.

"You're right," Illuminada said, mustering up the faint semblance of a rueful grin. "It's funny how I left the Church but still hang on to the guilt." She made a fist and pounded it on her chest as she spoke. "Once a breast beater, always a breast beater, I guess. Anyway, I expect you can get the kid to talk about what he heard. And keep him away from the cops, for a while at least." Illuminada still looked thoughtful.

"I'll do what I can. But in the meantime what about Betty? What if . . ." I couldn't bring myself to further articulate my fears for our friend's safety.

"We have to talk to Victor tomorrow," said Illuminada.

"Okay, I'll call up and make an appointment under some other name to arrange a funeral. That way he won't say anything to Betty about my visit. And since he won't know in advance that I'm coming to see him, he'll keep the appointment." I was relieved to have a plan; however, the picture of Betty with her head bashed in wouldn't go away.

"Okay. The only thing I can do is have someone

tail each of them." Illuminada was reaching for her cell phone as she spoke.

"And can't we put a little microphone or something into her bra so we can know if she needs help when they're alone? I mean no one can follow them into the sack." I thought it was a brilliant idea.

"Bel, you would have made a great spy." Illuminada was chuckling now. "*Dios mio*, can you imagine what Betty would do to us if we wired her and she ever found out? *We'd* need protection then."

Illuminada was right. I thought hard for a moment and then my words came out in a rush. "I have a better idea. If we want to make it hard for them to be alone, let's get Randy home from college for a week or so on some pretext. There's nothing that puts a damper on midlife romance like a college-age son in the house. I love Randy, but he's so used to being the center of Betty's universe that he'll rein her in just by being home." I couldn't keep the excitement out of my voice. This was a plan that would work.

"If we can just keep her out of trouble for another week, Randy will be home for spring break. That way we don't have to interfere with his education. Betty would never forgive us for that either." Illuminada paused a minute and added, "Besides, after you talk to Victor and he realizes that people are poking around Vallone and Sons, he'll be much less likely to brain Betty."

The only reason the sofa cushion I threw at Illuminada missed her head was that she had leaned over to pull on her boots. Instead it glanced off her shoulder and landed on the pile of pistachio shells, scattering them all over the floor.

Chapter 14

March 8, 1996

Dear Ma Bel,

It was good to talk to you the other night. It will take me a long time to realize that Grandpa Ike is really gone. You've had more than your share of sadness and worry lately.

Well at least you don't have to worry about me. I've met a terrific woman named Batsheva. She's beautiful and totally cool. She's already served in the army and she's really good for my Hebrew 'cause she doesn't speak much English.

You remember how I said I was going to do some traveling after the kibbutz? Well Batsheva says I can join this sort of unofficial army group for a week. You get to travel for free all over Israel, simulating army maneuvers. Awesome, huh? And then maybe Batsheva and I will go to the Golan Heights or Sinai for a holiday. We're totally psyched.

Well, I just finished digging an irrigation trench and a shower is in order.

Love,
Mark

P.S. And don't worry, I'm not even thinking of emigrating.

The Golan Heights? Isn't that a disputed territory? Will they travel there by bus? "Simulating army maneuvers?" "Emigrating?" Please God, don't let him get killed en route to the Golan Heights. And don't let him fall so hard for this Zionist GI Jane that he decides to emigrate and has to serve in the Israeli army. And don't let him marry her and stay there so I have to travel to Israel to see him and my poor grandchildren who will someday have to ride on Israeli buses and serve in the Israeli army. Please God . . .

I had ripped open Mark's letter, as always eager for his news, but by the time I finished reading it, I was more anxious than ever. If Ma didn't drive me over the edge, Mark and his ill-timed Israeli odyssey sure as hell would. It was almost a relief to file his letter and focus instead on my upcoming conference with Gilberto.

Fortunately he was coming at a time when I knew RECC would be buzzing with students and faculty. In the event that Gilberto Hernandez turned out to be Vinny's killer, I sure didn't want to be alone in the building with him.

When Gilberto arrived in my tiny office later that morning, he carried his book bag and a Styrofoam container of coffee. He didn't look like a killer today. He looked like a refugee from a GAP ad. "Have a seat, Gilberto." I smiled at the truly beautiful young man as he put his coffee on the desk and lowered his book bag to the floor. Gilberto's smooth features were expressionless, but I thought I detected a smoulder in his eyes that was at odds with his bland demeanor.

"Thanks, Professor Barrett. Mind if I finish this?" He held out the coffee container as he made his request.

"Not at all. I've got my tea. You can always count on that." I waved a hand at the thermal container on my desk. "Where did you disappear to when we were at the Met? I looked around to count heads and yours was missing. I was worried."

"Oh I just couldn't take it no more. You know Vinny used to talk about takin' the class to see the mummies and . . ." He looked down and then raised his head to say, "Sorry. I tol' Professor Simpson before I booked."

"Yes, I appreciate that," I said.

"Here. I better give you this before we get to talkin' about Vinny," said Gilberto, reaching into his bookbag and pulling out the latest draft of his research paper on trends in cremation, with a focus on rocketing one's "cremains" into space to become part of the cosmos.

"I think I got the works cited and stuff confused. Look." I glanced at the page he showed me and despaired. All the parenthetical references in the ten pages of text were wrong. Someday I planned to write an article entitled. "Teaching the Research Paper to Nontraditional Students: When a Citation Is Not a Parking Ticket."

Gilberto and I spent the next forty-five minutes reviewing how to cite sources in the text and how to list them at the end. I was relieved when he finally said wearily, "Okay. I'll give it another shot. I been havin' trouble concentratin' lately. I think I got it now. No problem." I flinched. Every time a student says "No problem," what he or she usually means is "I'm hopelessly confused. I have no idea what you've just explained."

Glberto had stuffed his book and paper back into his book bag by the time I reminded myself that we had more pressing matters to talk of than citations. I leaned back in my chair and said, "Gilberto, I'm sorry we didn't get to finish our conversation the other day. You seemed so upset. You were about to tell me what you heard the Vallone brothers arguing about. . . ." I paused, hoping Gilberto would, in fact, now tell me everything he had heard.

Gilberto laughed. Actually it was more of a snort, an ugly, sharp, nasal sound. Then lowering his head and with his eycs on the floor, he began speaking. His voice seemed to come out of the top of his head. "I tol' you. Victor was saying how Vinny shouldna spent the money their mother left him on a rock garden he had built in his backyard. He said he shoulda invested it. He called Vinny a lotta names on accounta that lousy rock garden." Gilberto hesitated and then, looking up and seeing that I had raised my eyebrows in inquiry, he added, "Said how he was a 'selfish little prick' and a disgrace to the memory of their parents. He was hard, man." Gilberto hung his head again, as if Victor's angry insults had been directed at him. When Gilberto next looked up, his perfectly proportioned features were creased in a grimace.

"Yes. He sounds hard. But what rock garden? I don't know about any rock garden." Again, I let my eyebrows ask the question.

"Vinny had a guy from New York, a landscape architect, design a real Japanese rock garden, ya know, with running water and everything, in his backyard.

It cost though. Really big bucks. It's nearly done. Vinny was real excited about it. He was plannin' to surprise everybody." Gilberto's mouth twitched into a line as he appeared to struggle with the feelings evoked by this particular memory.

"Including his brother?" I asked, directly this time.

"Yeah. I guess. But, hey man, it was his own money. His share of the money their mother left. It wasn't like he stole it." Gilberto looked indignant on behalf of his dead lover.

"You mentioned also that they had words about the business?" I asked, shifting the focus just a little.

"Somethin' about the caskets. I didn't stay to hear it all." Gilberto's eyes canvassed the office. He looked trapped. "No smokin' in here, right?"

"Right. But here. Have one of these. They sometimes help." I pushed my bowl of cellophane-wrapped butterscotch hard candies towards him, and he took one. I had to work quickly before Gilberto's need for nicotine drove him to the stairwell or the street.

"I guess you and Vinny never argued," I said innocently.

Again there was the bitter laugh. Then Gilberto sighed and said, "Yeah. We did. It was always the same thing." He sighed again and said wearily, "It was stupid, really. You know I'm graduatin' in June, right?" When I nodded, Gilberto continued, "Well, Vinny wanted me to stay on and work for Vallone and Sons and someday become a partner. . . ."

"That sounds reasonable. Why would that provoke an argument between you? Isn't that the dream job offer for an intern who is about to graduate?" *This is no time for your inner career counselor to butt in*, I rebuked myself. *Shut up and listen.*

There was that laugh again, and then Gilberto explained: "Except for one thing. Victor Vallone hates my guts. Vinny kept thinkin' that Victor would change his attitude toward me, but man, I didn't see it. After Vinny and I started . . .Victor was polite to me, but I know he tried to get Vinny to dump me. Vinny and I started arguin' about him and the two of them, they argued a lot about me." I couldn't tell if Gilberto was bragging or complaining.

"You know, Gilberto, I was surprised to hear that Victor and Vinny fought at all. I had always thought they got on well."

"He's the one who hit me. Gave me this." Gilberto gently fingered the faded yellow skin beneath his eye. The gesture distracted me for a moment from the fact that Gilberto's response to my question was something of a non sequitor. Clearly Gilberto was still smarting over Victor's animosity toward him.

"How awful. Why would he do that now that Vinny's dead?" I asked.

Gilberto shrugged. "I went back to Vinny's to get my stuff. I still had the key to his place, so I let myself in. I didn't think nothin' of it. I didn't hear Victor come in. When he saw me there in the house, he lost it, man. He hit me, took the key, and threw me out." He shook his head at the memory. "Don't you think I should tell the cops all this?"

"Do you think they'll believe you?" I wasn't entirely sure I believed him myself. I wanted to believe him, but there was something about this beautiful boy and his story that didn't sit quite right with me. I'd have to talk to Victor. But what I said aloud was, "You know, Gilberto, the Vallone family has been doing business in Jersey City for fifty years. They're very highly thought of. Why don't you wait until we see what the police come up with in the next few days? You can always go to the authorities later."

I waited a few seconds while he digested this advice. Then I asked, "Gilberto, do you know of anyone other than Victor who was angry at Vinny?"

Gilberto's face flushed a dark red and he glared at me as if I had just posed a really stupid question. "Professor Barrett, in this town a gay dude can get his head bashed in just for walkin' down the street."

Chapter 15

Dear Profesor Barrett,

Your Mom was feeling kind of down, so I took her by cab to the Grand Street Center where they have activities for the seniors. You know she ain't been able to go outside since she got here, but some of that snow melted this week. We gonna see about getting us some lunch while we out. Henry be through at the church by then so he drive us home. We probably be back before you get here, but this is just in case. Don't worry.

Very truly yours,
Pearl Hoskins

If one more person told me not to worry, I would scream. But I'd not scream at Pearl Hoskins. The woman was a saint and a genius. Of course Ma must be bored at home all day, but taking her out in the still snowy streets had seemed too risky to me. What if she fell? Besides, where would we go?

I hadn't thought of Ma as the Grand Street Center

type, but what do I know? I'd taught a dynamite creative writing class there once and noticed a lot of elderly folks sculpting. There had been a tai chi class going on too. Although I couldn't picture my mother, the card shark, molding clay or managing tai chi from her walker, I could see how an outing to the center would be a welcome change of scenery for her.

Because no one else had showed up for a scheduled meeting of the Curriculum Revision Committee, I got home early and so, for the first time in weeks, I had the house to myself. One morning last week, just as I was carefully folding myself from a shoulder stand into the plow, Ma had negotiated her walker through the bedroom doorway and over to the bed, where she sat, all the while talking a mile a minute.

"Ike, look at Sibyl. She's exercising. Did you ride your bike this morning, Ike?" How could she nag a dead man? How could I stretch and meditate when matricide was on my mind? But now, thanks to Pearl, I was alone at last. I immediately changed into sweats and a long-sleeved T-shirt, stretched out on the floor, and spent an uninterrupted hour doing hatha yoga.

I had just finished my last round of sun salutations and was letting my body merge with the floor while my mind floated somewhere between euphoria and sleep, when the phone rang. Off guard, I picked up the receiver without screening the call. "Bel? Beautiful? I was hoping I'd catch you. How're you holding up?"

My pulse raced when I heard the familiar husky voice. Sol always sounded like Louis Armstrong with a New York accent. "Oh Sol. How are you? Are you okay? When are you coming home?"

"Great. I'm great. But nothing definite yet about when I can leave. We're making headway each day.

Vaclav's playing everything slow and steady, and it's working." Deftly he changed the subject. "How are you and Sadie doing? I sent Rebecca a little 'get well' check the other day. I know she can't work yet. Mark still having a good time?"

"Sadie and I are doing okay. We just drive each other nuts, that's all. Mark's having a ball. He met a young woman, an Israeli. I'm a little worried he might want to stay there." I was a lot worried, actually.

"Well you'd be worried if he hadn't met a girl too, wouldn't you? Sounds like you're a few steps ahead on the worry timeline, as usual. Before I forget, what happened at the CCPW meeting? Did you go?" I was annoyed that Sol would think I hadn't gone, but I didn't want to carp long distance.

"Of course I went. They had some speakers from Paulus Hook. One of them used to be a student of mine. Before he took my class, he was afraid to speak in public and now . . ."

"When you get to heaven it will probably be full of your former students." Sol's rich chuckle wrapped itself around my heart. He always teased me about how often we ran into my students, and I realized I should save the story of Arthur Hoffman for another time.

Quickly I got back on track. "Marlene gave some tips on how to do a letter-writing campaign. I got copies of everything for you. CCPW is lobbying hard to get the light rail routed on the west side of town, away from the river. We're all supposed to write. There'll be plenty of work for you to do when you get back."

"Thanks for sitting in for me. I'm sure you had other things to do. Are you drowning in papers?" Sol also ribbed me about the amount of time I spent responding to student papers. Sure enough, he said, "Too bad you don't get paid by the word." He often muttered this line on weekend mornings as I sat reading essays while he wanted us to go to New York for brunch and a concert or a museum. Hearing the familiar words in the familiar voice, I wished away the miles between us. "Well beautiful, I'm glad I finally reached you. I'll run into another e-mail opportunity before too long. Give my best to Sadie. Remember, I love you."

As soon as I put down the phone, I realized that again I had not mentioned Vinny's murder. But, I asked myself rhetorically, why complicate his trip? Sol had wanted to return for my dad's funeral, but there hadn't been time. Now it didn't sound like he would be back for a while. And surely the Vinny business would be resolved before Sol left Prague. Things were finally beginning to happen.

My meeting with the surviving Vallone brother had convinced me of that.

"How do you do, Mrs. Howard? Have a seat, won't you? Tea? Coffee?"

"Tea please." I sat down in the Queen Ann chair Victor offered me.

"Teresa, two teas please. Mrs. Howard, I'm so sorry about the loss of your father." I was getting the full Vallone and Sons treatment, all right. This had been Vinny's job, actually. He had been the people person, the salesman. Victor worked behind the scenes keeping the books, hiring and firing, ordering supplies, and maintaining the facility. He did all the nitty-gritty stuff that kept the cash flowing, the staff competent, the prep room equipped, and the furniture polished. Vinny and his silver tongue had sold the services Victor provided.

At the moment, however, Victor was doing Vinny's job pretty well. He poured our tea and, as he handed me my cup, I said, "Actually, I'm not Mrs. Howard. I'm Bel Barrett, Vinny's colleague. You and I met briefly at his funeral, but I wouldn't expect you to remember me."

Victor's hand remained steady as he handed me my teacup. His eyes, however, widened momentarily, and then an equally momentary smile brightened his face. It was already gone when he spoke. "No. I was kind of out of it that day. But I remember my brother talking about you. And Betty talks about you all the time. But she didn't mention that you were coming." He tilted his head as if to ask why Betty hadn't cued him about my visit. "So Bel, why the charade? Sugar? Milk?"

When I shook my head, he sweetened his own tea and sat back in the chair he had taken behind his desk. I said pointedly, "Betty doesn't know I'm here. Illuminada Guttierez does though." Teresa had left the room after serving our tea. She was probably at her own desk in the anteroom. At least I hoped she was.

"What's going on?" Victor asked, a trace of impatience sharpening his tone.

"Okay." I took a deep breath. "As Betty's told you, she, Illuminada, and I are trying to figure out who killed Vinny. Gilberto Hernandez said—"

I got no further. Victor replaced his teacup precisely in the center of the saucer and began to speak, spitting each word out through clenched teeth. " 'Gilberto Hernandez says . . .' What does that conniving little shit say? That my brother gave him HIV? That he tried to blackmail us? That last week I caught him in Vinny's house making off with Vinny's stuff like the greedy little psycho he is? That I hit him? Yeah. I hit him. I should have killed him."

Victor stopped speaking as if surprised by his own outburst. His face now looked as expressionless as I remembered it from Vinny's funeral. His next words were curt, businesslike. "I'm sorry. . . . Please forgive both my interruption and my language, Professor. You were saying . . ." Somehow Victor had taken control of himself and our conversation. Now I was being questioned.

I had little choice but to respond. "What Gilberto actually said was that he overheard an argument between you and Vinny shortly before Vinny was murdered."

As soon as I paused for breath, Victor resumed interrogating me. At least that's what it felt like. "Let me get this straight, Professor. You sneak into my office pretending to be a client because Gilberto Hernandez told you he overheard me arguing with my brother?"

"Well . . ." I sputtered.

"A simple yes or no. Is that why you came here?"

I nodded.

"So you think *I* killed Vinny?" The man was an inquisitor.

"It's possible," I answered softly, eyeing the door and listening for the sound of the word processor or Teresa's voice.

"And so you're worried about Betty, right? You're afraid she's getting involved with a murderer?" I had to hand it to him. He had moved from point A to point B remarkably quickly. He stood up now and walked around the desk.

"Well, now that you mention it, Illuminada and I are concerned, yes," I said, standing up and looking him straight in the eye. "And I'm not about to apologize for that either." And then before he could turn the tables on me again, I pressed him. "What's this about Vinny giving Gilberto HIV? Are you saying that Vinny was HIV positive and that he infected Gilberto?" Even as I spoke, I heard Joevelyn's words—*You know, maybe he got bad news or somethin', like, you know, his health*—echoing in my head.

"I'm saying that's what Hernandez told me. The little vulture tried to blackmail me. Said he tested HIV positive and that it was Vinny's fault. Wanted me to pay him not to "expose" Vinny, as he put it. Said for the right price he'd go away and go into treatment."

"*Was* Vinny HIV positive?" I asked simply, reaching into my bag for a Post-it. If I could remember to ask her, Illuminada could get that information out of some lab tech somewhere. I'd bet my estrogen patch on it.

"I doubt it, but if he was, it was Hernandez who infected him. Before he fell for that little creep, Vinny had been a poster boy for safe sex. He even wore a condom when he read about sex, for Christ's sake." Victor's voice lowered. He looked worn and tired.

"*Did* you and Vinny argue a lot?" I refused to let my sympathy for him prevent me from getting what I had come for.

"Of course. I'm the older brother. I've been looking out for Vinny all my life. And that wasn't always an easy job. Especially after our mother died, when he really came out of the closet. He got a little crazy. That's when he got involved with Hernandez, a pretty gold digger half his age who had Vinny wrapped around his little finger from the start. Then with that house . . ." Here Victor scratched his head.

"You mean the Japanese garden?" I asked innocently.

"That's just part of it. He put every dime he made into that place. I didn't say much at first because I figured it was a good investment. But then he took all the money my mother left him and had that garden put in. . . . He should have saved some of that money. We're not getting any younger." Victor shook his head, perhaps recalling that now Vinny would never need to worry about saving for retirement. "But no. He had to have that goddamn garden. It doesn't even have any flowers in it. For chrissake, my brother has a pile of rocks behind his house that cost fifty grand. Can you believe that?" Victor shrugged his shoulders and turned his palms up in a classic gesture of incredulity.

"Did you fight about the business too?" I might as well go for it all.

"Only recently. About the caskets. I want to change our policy and give clients the choice of obtaining their own coffin or getting one through us. There's a big markup on coffins they get through us, even the cheapest ones. Vinny wanted things to stay the same. My baby brother was most ethical when it wouldn't cost him anything." Victor practically spat out the phrase "baby brother." It was clear that he was still at odds with his sibling. "Now, if there's nothing else, Professor. I am trying to run a business here." Victor was seated at his desk again, leafing through papers.

"Well, I'm sorry to hold you up, but you mentioned that you caught Gilberto stealing at Vinny's? Was that why you hit him?" I wanted to compare Victor's version of this episode with Gilberto's.

"I went over there to meet a realtor. I have to do something about renting or selling Vinny's place. It's got a huge mortgage. When I got there, I heard a noise in the bedroom. There was Hernandez going through Vinny's dresser drawers and throwing stuff into a suitcase. I didn't wait for an explanation. Now that I think of it, I should have called the cops. But it felt really good to mess up that pretty face myself. Is that all?"

"Just one more thing. Why didn't you tell Betty about your argument with your brother and about hitting Gilberto?"

"Professor Barrett, I have met only one woman who interested me since my divorce five years ago, and that's Betty Ramsey. I'm trying to make a good impression on her, so I haven't told her all about my foul temper yet. Do you blame me?" With that question, he pushed a button on his desk and said, "Teresa, will you please show Mrs. Howard out?"

It was only after Teresa had escorted me out that I contemplated the fact that Victor might tell Betty all about my visit over a glass of the house red in some local bistro that very night. But then again, he might not.

Ma's trip to the Grand Street Center with Pearl had been well worth the cab fare. "You know Sibyl, I bet Pearl and I were the only ones at the center who weren't Italian, right Pearl?"

Pearl's eyes twinkled just a little when, without missing a beat, she answered, "Right, Miz Bickoff. But you could probably pass if you put your mind to it."

Without acknowledging Pearl's dig, Ma went on. "I couldn't believe that woman, Sofia was her name maybe. Remember the woman who said she had known Frank Sinatra's mother?" Ma was looking at Pearl now for a sign of affirmation. When Pearl nodded, Ma went on. "She was doing all those exercises and she's older than I am. I bet you a dollar I could do some of those exercises sitting in a chair, what do you think, Pearl?"

"I'd like to see them try and stop you," Pearl answered, giving Ma a hug. Ma was chattering right through the hug, but Pearl didn't seem to mind. "And I met Pearl's grandson. He drove us home and helped me inside. Such a nice young man. So serious and well mannered. He says he has you for a teacher." Ma was sitting in the kitchen while Pearl was getting ready to leave.

Ma had been talking nonstop since she entered the room behind her walker, but not once had she addressed Lenny or my dad. It wasn't until later that evening when I tucked her into bed that she said, "Your father couldn't get over the snowman in front of your house. Did Lenny make that with the children?"

After flicking on the night-light in her room, I went to the front door and peered out. My breath caught and my body stiffened. There in the moonlight was a large snowman. Or was it a snowwoman? When I went out the next morning, I saw that the creature was wearing a watch-plaid scarf and had blue M&M eyes and held a frozen, blood red rose in one hand.

Chapter 16

To: Caregiverssupportgroup@sos.com
From: Bbarrett@circle.com
Re: Mommie Dearest
Date: 03/10/96 23:24:06

Thanks Suzanne, Heidi, and Merrill for the list of geriatric shrinks in the metropolitan area. One of them had a cancellation so I actually managed to make an appointment for my mother during my spring break next week. But guess what? My mother refuses to go. Here is this poor woman talking nonstop to anyone who will listen, especially her husband, who's dead, and mine, whom I divorced years ago, and she won't go to a shrink. "Sibyl, you know how I feel about psychiatrists. They just take your money. Remember when you went to that psychiatrist and you got from her the idea of getting a divorce? Well, your father and I don't want a divorce. So why should I go to a psychiatrist?" Or she says, "There's nothing wrong with me except my knees. Is a psychiatrist going to help me walk?" I did persuade her to go for a physical to an internist with a geriatric practice, and I hope he can help her. I don't see how though. She's refused knee surgery every time a doctor has suggested it.

Any ideas on how to get her to a shrink?

"How's your mom? Has she seen the shrink yet?" I wasn't really in the mood for Betty's opening line, but I was relieved that she was still talking to me. Maybe Victor hadn't mentioned my visit. Well, no matter. Earlier, during a hurried phone conversation, Illuminada and I had agreed to tell Betty our concerns about Victor. After all, Betty was a big girl, and if she got mad, she got mad. Getting mad was better than getting dead.

I had completely forgotten that the snowperson was still in front of the house until Illuminada quipped, "I see you're into outsider art," as she shed her parka.

"Very funny," I replied, making a face and taking the parka. "Give me your jacket, Betty," I barked. I draped each coat on a different dining-room chair, not even worrying about their frosting of snow dripping on the hardwood floor. The three of us sat around the other end of the table, passing the sherry bottle until all our glasses were filled. I nuked some of the spaghetti with clam sauce I'd made Ma for dinner. We sopped up the garlicky gravy with slabs of bread so good that Frank Sinatra used to have it flown from Hoboken to Hollywood.

I really wanted to get into and past telling Betty about Victor, so as soon as we had pushed our plates away, I began to edge toward it. "I spent almost an hour with Gilberto Hernandez on Tuesday, and Vic was right." Betty was reaching for her personal digital assistant, the handheld computer for which she had forsworn her trusty laptop. "He and Vinny *were* lovers. Gilberto is grieving. He's bitter. He's angry. And he can't document research worth a damn. I don't know what to make of him except . . ."

"Except what?" asked Betty, her fingers poised over

her machine. Damn Illuminada. She was leaving the dirty work to me.

"Except that Gilberto said he overheard a major argument between the Vallone brothers shortly before Vinny's death." I paused because Betty's fingers had stopped moving over her mini-keyboard.

She was staring at me. "Say what, girl?" Her voice was half serious and half joking. "What are you trying to say, Bel?"

"She's saying that Victor Vallone is a murder suspect, Betty." Finally Illuminada weighed in, softening her words by reaching over to touch Betty's shoulder.

Betty shook off Illuminada's hand and snapped, "No. Vic would never . . . What the hell are you two talking about?" She made no pretense of typing now, but looked from me to Illuminada. "What's going on?"

"Gilberto told me Victor was furious because Vinny used his share of their mother's legacy to build a Japanese rock garden with fountains in his backyard."

"You don't think Vic murdered his brother over a garden, do you?" Sarcasm lent bite to Betty's question.

"There's more," said Illuminada quietly. I really hated seeing Betty suffer, hated watching her try to both absorb and deny news that might save her life by killing a relationship that had promised so much.

I took a deep breath. "They also fought over changing the funeral home's policy on caskets." Somewhere in the middle of my explanation, I stopped because Betty was again looking from me to Illuminada, bewilderment reflected in her darting eyes.

"Whoa! Now you're saying that Vic bashed in his brother's skull over a bunch of caskets? That's what you expect me to believe?" Although Betty's voice had softened, there was no mistaking the anger behind her words.

"Don't be naive, Betty," scolded Illuminada. "You know as well as I do that those boxes are the bread and butter of the funeral business." I could tell from her voice that she was appealing to Betty's common sense and smarts in the hope of providing temporary pain relief.

"Gilberto also accused Victor of giving him a black eye," I added, feeling like a creep even as the words left my mouth.

"Gilberto? You're going to believe Gilberto over Vic? I don't get it. Gilberto probably made all this up to protect himself." Now she was staring at Illuminada as if she had given up all hope of a sensible explanation from me. "The least you could do is talk to Vic, give him a chance to explain all these allegations. . . ." I thought it was a good sign that Betty was problem solving once again.

"Betty, I hope you don't shoot the messenger, but I did talk to Vic this afternoon. He confirmed everthing Gilberto said and added a few wrinkles, mostly about Gilberto trying to blackmail him." Betty lowered her head onto her folded arms. At first I thought she was crying, but she was too quiet and still. I took a deep breath before I continued, "Illuminada and I don't want you to get hurt." Too late, I realized the folly of my words. Betty was already hurt. "You know what I mean," I added lamely.

Suddenly Betty raised her head and said, "Illuminada, why don't you find somebody who'll tell you if Vic has an alibi for the night Vinny was killed? And Gilberto Hernandez too." It was a further good sign that Betty was once again delegating tasks, but this one sounded like a final desperate effort to exonerate Victor.

"I asked my former client Faith about that the other day, right after Bel and I talked. Faith's an office manager in Homocide now, but she still remembers what I did for her. She scanned police reports of their initial interviews with Victor and Gilberto. The reports indicate that both have alibis, but—"

Betty's relief was evident in her smile. "Praise the Lord. I knew Vic—"

"*Chiquita*, hold on." Illuminada's tone was stern. "Nobody in Homicide bothered to check those alibis because they were too busy interviewing Henry Granger. The problem is that Gilberto Hernandez and Victor Vallone have the same alibi."

Both Betty and I looked mystified, so Illuminada continued: "Each one of them claims to have been working late at Vallone and Sons that evening. Gilberto says he was in the prep room and Victor says he was in his office."

"So they could both have been there and not even seen each other, or one could have been there and not the other or neither one could have been there, is that what you're saying?" I asked, watching Betty's face fall.

"That and—*dios mio*, why should either one of them provide an alibi for the other? There's no love lost between them," Illuminada explained. She sounded exasperated.

When Betty looked up, her eyes were glistening, but she spoke with resolution. "Okay. I should have known better than to get into this thing with Vic in the first place." With just a hint of a tremble in her lips, she squared her shoulders and announced, "Okay, I won't see him alone anymore until this is settled. It was too much too soon anyway. If he cares at all, he'll understand. If he doesn't . . ." She shrugged. I could hardly stand watching Betty "Ramrod" Ramsey, control freak extraordinaire, pay such a heavy price for falling in love. It wasn't fair.

"What about Eleanor Chambers? Or is Victor the only suspect we're serious about now?" asked Betty. I forgave her the sarcasm. She was having a tough night.

"No. There's Eleanor and I'm not writing off Henry Granger either. *Caramba* Bel, don't jump all over me." Illuminada was reacting to the look of surprise and annoyance that I couldn't keep from contorting my face. "I know you're fond of his grandmother, and I know you think he's reformed, but . . . I'm just keeping an open mind, that's all."

"Right. I'm glad for you." Actually, I wanted to strangle her, and she knew it. Frankly, Pearl Hoskins's news that Henry was consorting with an old gang member from his past, combined with Henry's moodiness, had chipped away just a little at my certainty about his innocence. That made Illuminada's suspicion of him that much harder to ignore. "Now just tell me about Eleanor, please." I was really impatient.

But Illuminada, usually the one who tapped her fingers and looked at her watch so often that Betty had once asked her if she wore it during sex, was not to be hurried tonight. "Before I tell you what I dug up about your friend Eleanor, there is one other suspect we have to check out: Hattie Majors. I know she's a real long shot, but we have to eliminate all the possibilities." Illuminada looked serious and tired. I wasn't the only one with a wicked schedule. I tried to focus attentively on what she was saying. It was hard.

"So tell us. What's the deal with Batty Hattie? That's who you're raggin' on now isn't it?" Betty looked impatient too.

"I have nothing to say. I know Bel talked to her. I'll poke around about her too," said Illuminada. I caught the end of her sentence as I brought in a plate of Camembert and some pears from the kitchen and set it on the table. Perhaps slicing the fruit would calm me down.

"Anybody want tea or decaf instead of sherry?" I asked as pleasantly as I could.

As I poured the decaf, I said, "So now will you *please* tell me what you've been able to find out about Eleanor Chambers?" The way I practically shouted "please" made my request more like an order than I'd intended. I tried to soften my mandate by explaining, "She's driving me crazy. Between her out there and my mom in here, I can't take much more."

"You're so attractive when you whine, Bel," was Betty's snide response. I recognized Betty's dig as a sign that she no longer blamed me for the lousy turn her love life had taken. I flashed her a smile.

"Yeah. I just love it when you go into your Jewish Princess routine. Illuminada too was aware of the significance of Betty's remark. "*Dios mio*, between you and the African Queen over there"—Illuminada waved her pear slice at Betty before going on—"I feel like, you know, so mellow compared to the two of you." Only after she saw Betty smile did Illuminada begin to share what she'd learned about Eleanor. "Well, I checked area hospitals and police."

"Why police? They aren't even suspicious of her." I was worried. I didn't want any police involved until we had some hard evidence.

"I wanted to see if there have been any restraining

orders issued on her in the past. I figured if she's stalking you and she stalked Vinny, she probably has a record. And she does." Illuminada's smile revealed her satisfaction. "All right, all right. I'm going to tell you. Of course I could be like you and drag this story out for a year or two. . . ."

When I made a face at her, Illuminada poured herself some more decaf and resumed speaking. "Anyway, it turns out that she had a restraining order issued on her in the Village a few years ago for stalking her minister. And she violated that restraining order so often that she was admitted to the psych ward at St. Luke's for thirty days of treatment to be followed by outpatient therapy. When she got out, she moved to Jersey City and got a job at a florist's. Floral Tribute's the name of it. As soon as she started working and had some health insurance, she began treatment. And—"

"Were you able to get a hold of her shrink?" I was excited now.

"Bel, no shrink is going to talk about a patient. That would be a breach of confidentiality." Here Illuminada paused.

"But suppose the patient is dangerous." I shuddered at the thought that when my two friends left later in the evening, Eleanor would very likely be lurking somewhere near my house, her eyes glued to the windows and door, her boots leaving prints in the lightly falling snow.

"Doesn't matter. The shrink would be obligated to warn a specific individual Eleanor has actually threatened to harm, but the shrink still wouldn't discuss her case with others."

"Great. So she has confidentiality and I have *agita*," I muttered.

"Keep your pants on, Bel." Betty was typing again now, but I could see she was not happy with Illuminada's narrative pacing. It would be only a matter of moments before she would assert herself and take control of the conversation. I was right. Turning to Illuminada, Betty said, "Illuminada Guttierrez, get on with it. I'm serious, girl."

"Okay. Okay. So there I am trying to figure out who I could get to hack into St. Luke's computer system to get a diagnosis. Then we could take it from there. And, let me tell you *chiquitas*, I was worried about doing this because whatever we did get illegally like that, we couldn't use as evidence. *Como mierda*, I was all bent out of shape over the ethics of hacking too. Then I remembered Fatima."

"All right Illuminada. I'll play your silly game. Who's Fatima?" Why did everything have to be so complicated?

Illuminada went on. "Fatima Pantojal is a physicians' supervisor at SECURE, the HMO Raoul and I joined last year. You remember? Oh, I'm sorry. You probably don't remember." Before Illuminada's sideswipe at my postmenopausal memory, I had wanted to kill her. After that remark I wanted to kill her slowly and painfully. Illuminada was continuing. "Anyway, I told you. We're both self-employed, so we have to arrange our own health insurance. I did some work for Fatima when her boy was being beaten up every day on the way home from school. When I asked her about insurance, she sent an agent to see us and we ended up going with SECURE."

"It's not that I'm not passionately interested in your family's health insurance, Illuminada, but give me a break and get to the point." I was rolling my eyes now, all pretense of politeness gone. Betty had collapsed over her computer, simulating sleep.

"Well, the gist of what Fatima told me was that if you're in certain HMOs, there's really no such thing as patient confidentiality." Illuminada proclaimed this news with unrestrained glee, which seemed oddly out of keeping with the news itself.

"Say what?" I was glad Betty didn't understand either.

Illuminada's eyes positively glowed as she spelled it out. "Fatima told me that after a certain number of sessions with a particular patient, the shrink has to fill out a preauthorization form, sort of a progress report including a diagnosis, a prognosis, a summary of the course of treatment, a risk assessment, and the current mental status of the patient. The shrink submits these to the HMO in order to get authorization to continue to treat the patient for another set of sessions. The office workers who see these reports aren't really under the same obligation to observe confidentiality with regard to their content as a shrink is. They're paper pushers." Illuminada sat back and smiled. That woman just loves it when she gets what she wants.

In spite of myself, I was interested in Illuminada's revelations. But I was more interested in worming Eleanor's diagnosis out of her. "So tell us, supersleuth, how did you figure out what HMO Eleanor belongs to and get the diagnosis? Because I know you did."

"Flattery will get you everywhere, Bel. I got her social security number from the RECC registrar because I'd never thought to get it from you. Then I gave it to Fatima and she checked SECURE first. It wasn't there. That would have been too easy. So I called Floral Tribute, you know, where Eleanor works. I said I was an agent for an HMO called

FAITH and tried to sell them a small business policy. The owner told me they already work with TRUST. After I told Fatima that, she called a supervisor she knows at TRUST who used to work with her at SECURE and found a preauthorization form written for Eleanor." Here Illuminada paused just a second before she said, "You might want to think about getting a restraining order yourself. Eleanor Chambers is an erotomanic with a history of risk behavior that includes previous hospitalization and violent ideation."

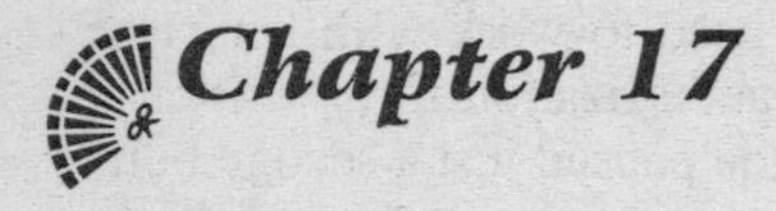

Chapter 17

Diagnostic criteria for 297.1 Delusional Disorder

A. Nonbizarre delusions (i.e., involving situations that occur in real life, such as being followed, poisoned, infected, loved at a distance, or deceived by spouse or lover, or having a disease) of at least one month's duration.

Erotomanic Type. *This subtype applies when the central theme of the delusion is that another person is in love with the individual. The delusion often concerns idealized romantic love and spiritual union rather than sexual attraction. The person about whom this conviction is held is usually of higher status (e.g., a famous person or a superior at work), but can be a complete stranger. Efforts to contact the object of the delusion (through telephone calls, letters, gifts, visits, and even surveillance and stalking) are common. . . . Most individuals with this subtype in clinical samples are female; most individuals with this subtype in forensic samples are male. Some individuals with this subtype, particularly males, come into conflict with the law in their efforts to* *pursue the object of their delusion or in their misguided efforts to "rescue" him or her from some imagined danger.*

I practically wet my pants the day the Funeral Service Ed class convened for their last session before spring break. The first drafts of their research papers were due, so students were rummaging through their book bags to retrieve them. I was routinely noting absences in my roll book. When I looked up, Eleanor Chambers was taking a seat near the back of the center section.

I had not had time to do more than scan the printouts on erotomania that Illuminada had handed me or to consider the implications of getting a restraining order. But here was the woman who had been leaving me weird phone messages, odd packages, even odder notes, and who had built that bizarre snow sculpture at my home. Right in front of me was the lunatic who had been stalking me for weeks, the same woman who had a history of stalking others, the woman who had been stalking Vinny and who might very well have bashed his head in. I was not only scared out of my wits but also out of the compassion I customarily feel in response to troubled students.

I forced myself to approach her and say quietly, "Eleanor, we need to talk about your attendance and missed work. Please stay after class for a moment." The other students were, of course, all ears to see how I would handle the reappearance of a student who had missed most of the semester.

They were disappointed when I waited after class until everyone had left. I had deliberately positioned myself in the open doorway as they filed out. There was no way I was going to be behind a closed door alone in a classroom with Eleanor Chambers, thank you very much. I resolved to limit our conversation to Eleanor's attendance and her obvious need for counseling. Now that I knew she had been issued restraining orders in at least two places, I was more wary than ever of setting her off. I was equally wary of leading her on. "Eleanor, you know you've only been to three classes this semester, and you haven't turned in any work to either me or to Professor Simpson. I assume something is preventing you from accomplishing your educational goals, and again, I'd like you to talk to a counselor. . . ."

I paused. Eleanor, who stood awkwardly about a foot away from me, looked at the floor and then said defiantly, "That's not what Professor Vallone says. He says I should talk to you. He knows how you really feel about me." She raised her head and stared straight into my eyes.

Stunned by her words, I was about to retort, "Professor Vallone has been dead for almost two months," when I pictured my mother and recalled the folly of reasoning with somebody delusional. And Eleanor was deluded as hell. Not only was she imagining that I had romantic feelings for her, but now she had convinced herself that Vinny was still alive and talking to her. This was a new and yet all too familiar wrinkle.

I didn't want her to get any more upset than she already was, so I repeated quietly, "Eleanor, you've missed a lot of classes, and you need to discuss your academic status with a counselor." Then, leaving the tall, angular figure standing alone in the open doorway, I escaped into the throng of students passing in the hall.

I was, as usual, drawn into the demands of the rest of the teaching day, which distracted me from my run-in with Eleanor. I had one more class that day, a Speech class in which the students were, to put it kindly, less than attentive. It was speech rehearsal day and they were working in pairs, listening to one another's speeches and providing feedback. Usually this activity filled them with purpose and urgency, but that day, as I circulated among the pairs, I overheard lots of chatter about plans for spring break.

I couldn't blame them. Even though I planned to spend the next week reading student papers, taking my mother to the doctor, catching up on my graduate-school work, researching erotomania, and answering condolence cards, I was still looking forward to the hiatus from RECC. We were all ready for a break from classes and from winter as well.

Determined to make the most of every vacation moment, on the way home I picked up a chicken, a few potatoes, some carrots and broccoli, and a tape of *Inherit the Wind*, one of Ma's all-time favorite movies. Even though her days as the fastest court stenographer in Brooklyn were long gone, she still loved courtroom dramas. I was relieved that there was no floral offering from Eleanor to sidestep when I crossed the threshold. But there was another surprise.

I heard Sol before I got to the kitchen, where I found Henry Granger effortlessly holding him by the armpits at least a foot off the floor, while dodging the older man's kicks. At first I had the mad thought that they were locked together in some sort of dance. But Henry's expression was grim, and Sol, ignoring the peril of his position, was red-faced and yelling, "I don't care who you are. You don't belong here. Get the hell out before I call the cops! Go on! Move!"

I screamed, "Sol! Henry! Stop! What are you doing? What's the matter? Stop!"

Henry's glower relaxed slightly when he saw me. Smoothly he deposited the love of my life on the floor in front of me the way Virginia Woolf had once gifted me with a dead robin. Then, jerking his head in Sol's direction, Henry said, "Yo, Profesor Barrett. This dude, he got in widout me even knowin' he was here. You want him gone or what?" If I had nodded, Henry would have ousted Sol without breaking a sweat.

"Oh no Henry. This is Sol Hecht. He lives here. He's been away. Henry, where's your grandmother? Is my mother okay? Is something wrong?"

"My grandmother, she started coughin' and snifflin' this mornin.' Thought she was comin' down wid somethin,' so she beep me and ask me to come over after class and stay with Miz Bickoff so she could go home early. Your mother's havin' a nap." As he spoke, Henry picked up his jacket from a kitchen chair and moved toward the door.

"Sol, this is Hen . . ." I turned toward Sol but stopped when I saw his face.

"Thanks for your help today, Henry. And please tell your grandmother I hope she feels better," I called to Henry's retreating figure.

I turned back to face Sol. "Sol!" I cried out. Sol was picking up his duffel bag and walking toward the front door. He still wore his coat. Dumping my groceries on the kitchen table, I ran after him. "What is it, Sol? I can explain about Henry."

To my immense relief, Sol turned and spoke. But each syllable felt like an arrow in my heart. "Yes, Bel,

I'm sure you can explain why, when I come home, some hoodlum with his hits branded all over his face is sprawled in my kitchen as if he owns the place. And I'm sure you can also explain why your mother is apparently here alone with this thug. Granted, Sadie Bickoff's not one of my favorite people, but Jesus, Bel, she's your mother. She deserves better than to be acting out your version of *Driving Miss Daisy* with some refugee from *Boyz N the Hood.*

I started to speak, but Sol held up his hand and continued his staccato monologue. "No, Bel. It's my nickel. Maybe you *can* explain why when I walk in I find this on our doorstep. Sol reached into his coat pocket and pulled out a handful of white rose petals and a crumpled wad of paper. As he peeled open the paper, rose petals fluttered to the floor around his feet. Oblivious, he read, " 'I'll prove I'm right about everything. You'll see. I thank God for bringing us together.' I'm sure you *can* explain all this, Bel," Sol went on with a sneer. "But don't bother. I can read the signs. You're involved in some misguided rescue mission again. None of this is what I signed on for." He waved his arm around the room and the gesture somehow took in the now absent Henry Granger as well as the rose petals underfoot.

"I thought we were sharing our lives. But if we were, I wouldn't have to be mauled by an obvious gangster you're probably befriending for some *cockamamie* reason. Get real, Bel. It's not like we haven't been down this road before. I thought we had an agreement. I played fair, and you didn't. I'm outta here." And he was. Just like that.

I stood in the living room still wearing my coat. Just as I was about to start bawling, I heard the familiar sound of metal wheels against the wood floor, and there was Ma, a vision in her burgundy knit pant-suit with a jaunty burgundy-and-white silk scarf around her neck. Clinging to the rail of her walker with her tiny veined hands, she looked around. Seeing me, she said brightly, "Oh Sibyl, it's you. I could've sworn I heard a man yelling. But your father's asleep and Lenny's at work. I must be imagining things."

Chapter 18

TOUGH LOVE FOR ESSEX STREETERS FROM LIGHT RAIL ENTHUSIAST

I totally understand the feelings of the home and condo owners of Essex Street who will be living in close proximity to the train itself. Those doomed denizens of Essex Street are flummoxed by the prospect of a high-tech, high-speed electric train wreaking havoc on their serene street. Nonetheless I remain absolutely wedded to the progressive plan to route the Light Rail through Paulus Hook. It will connect our little corner of Jersey City with vital centers of commerce and industry and thus be a boon to the neighborhood. The route through Essex Street disrupts far fewer residents than would be affected by other proposed routes. Therefore I urge you unfortunate inhabitants of the benighted block to comfort yourselves with the gratitude and appreciation of your fellow citizens of Paulus Hook. . . .

Jane Q. Public
Jersey City

If Sol hadn't left, I might never have found this letter. That was slim consolation. I was used to Sol being away, but I had never felt abandoned before. His angry words had hit home. The night Sol walked out I cried myself to sleep hugging Virginia Woolf.

But I couldn't sleep long. I woke up terrified in the middle of a nightmare about M&M bags filled with white rose petals. Once awake, I kept rehashing that scene in the kitchen with Sol and Henry and Sol's final accusations. Why *hadn't* I told Sol about Vinny in the first place? Was I, in fact, punishing him for being away so much? Was my subconscious nothing more than a vindictive inner bitch? When I couldn't stand the inside of my own head anymore, I got out of bed, seeking distraction from my demons. After all, for denial queens, a little introspection goes a long way.

Wide awake, I decided to review my graduate-school notes in preparation for a conference I had scheduled with Professor Holland during RECC's spring break. Propped up on pillows and with the light on, I felt less vulnerable to my own guilt. I pored over my notebook and when I came to Vinny's teaching journals, I sighed and began to reread them too.

Suddenly I tensed. What I was reading reminded me of something else. What the hell was it? I reread the journal passage that had triggered the would-be memory. Vinny's florid phrases were all there, and a myriad of alliterations too. Vinny's writing was, in some ways, like a lot of adolescent writing, a kind of cross between the ecstacies of Anne Frank and the agonies of Holden Caufield.

When the memory finally bubbled up, I thought about it for a few minutes. Then I climbed out of bed and rummaged through the stacks of mail on Sol's desk. I found what I was looking for, the letters Marlene Proletariat had read aloud at the CCPW meeting. They were still right where I'd put them after the meeting. Quickly I leafed through them, scanning each one and moving on until I found the one I wanted.

Even though this letter was signed Jane Q. Public, I was willing to bet that it had been written by Vinny. I mean, could there be another person who wrote like that? And if Vinny did write that letter, there was a whole new area of my late colleague's life to check out. Illuminada's insistence on covering all bases echoed in my head. It wouldn't be too hard either. I could do it myself.

I spent the weekend struggling to impose order on my mother's affairs. I filled four sheets of a yellow legal pad with lists of calls to make, questions to ask, forms to complete. I wanted to get my father's will probated, his estate settled and to pay the condo mortgage and other bills Ma had from Charleston. My own credit card bills had come in swollen with my cross-country travel and my father's funeral expenses. My savings account was diminishing, and Rebecca had just e-mailed, asking for a loan for tuition and expenses since she couldn't wait tables until her cast came off.

I felt so bad that one night after Ma went to bed, I got out the Ziploc bags containing all the bags of M&M's that Eleanor had ever sent. Illuminada had advised me to hang on to them in case we ever needed to have them fingerprinted or something. I sat alone in the kitchen in the dark and, after carefully dividing the candies into the monochromatic piles I had delighted in making as a child, I ate every last one. At that point, I needed chocolate more than evidence.

In fact, this guilty nocturnal infusion proved inspiring. I awoke the next day determined to follow through on my latest insight, even if it turned out to be way off base. I called Sarah Wolf, managing editor at the *Jersey City Herald.* Sarah remains a close friend of mine in spite of the fact that she is already the grandmother of an enchanting toddler while I have an empty lap. It was never easy to get through to Sarah at the newspaper office, but I knew her extension and was able to put off the intern screening her calls by telling him that if he didn't let me speak to Sarah immediately, he might find himself delivering *Herald*s in Kearny instead of getting coffee and fielding calls for Sarah.

"Hi Bel. Good to hear your voice. I'm so sorry about your dad. I know you and your mom must be having quite a time of it." Sarah's condolence card was among those I had been meaning to answer, her calls among those I'd had no time to return. Her next words made me smile. "I haven't seen you in ages. A dinner reunion would be super. Shall I get my book?" I silently thanked God that her recent promotion hadn't made Sarah snooty any more than being a grandma had turned her into one of those stroller-pushing, photo-carrying braggarts I so envied.

I said, "Of course we can make a dinner date, but give me a couple of weeks, okay?"

"Sure. Did Sol make it back yet? All this waterfront development in the county must be driving him crazy."

Before I started to sniffle, I said in that shorthand that close friends can decode, "Long story, Sarah. Over dinner. In the meantime, I need a favor, and I need it pretty soon."

Sarah was all business now. "Do you want to tell

me over the phone? I bet I know what you're sticking your nose into now. I love it when you play cops and robbers, Bel. I'm not saying a word though, so just tell me what you want."

"Sarah, what's the *Herald*'s policy on letters to the editor? Don't they all have to be signed even if the author uses a pseudonym or wants the letter published anonymously?" The answer I got was the one I'd been hoping for.

"Yes. That's not every paper's policy, but it is ours," Sarah replied. "Is that all you wanted? That was easy." I heard her chuckle on the other end of the phone. She knew damn well I wanted something more.

"No, Sarah. I want a big favor. I need to know the real name of the author of a letter to the editor from November twelfth, nineteen ninety-five, signed Jane Q. Public. Can you get that for me?" I was sure she could. The question was, would she. "I promise, Sarah, whatever happens, I'll protect my sources."

Laughing, she said, " You must be feeling better. You know what I want in return, right?"

I laughed too. "You got it, Sarah. You'll get the story first. I promise."

"Should I call you or just e-mail it?"

Chapter 19

To: Caregiverssupportgroup@sos.com
From: Bbarrett@circle.com
Re: Maybe a Miracle
Date: 03/19/96 08:26:30

Well, thank you Vicki. The trip to Dr. De Cento was a success. You're right. The man *is* a miracle worker. He spent over an hour talking to my mother alone. Then he examined her for another half hour. He took a lot of blood and gave her a really good workup. She was her usual chatty self but surprisingly cooperative. Dr. De Cento is such a good listener. He was really gentle and patient.

When they finished, he invited me to join them in his office and told me that he was taking my Mom off Valium. It was prescribed on the night my father died by the doctor who lived next door to her in Charleston. De Cento wants to see if the Valium is what's confusing her. Could that be? Ma was very agreeable.

He said there is a new nonsurgical procedure that may help her osteoarthritis, some kind of shot involving gel. I can't believe it. And Ma didn't say no to this either. At least not yet. We're going back in a month for a follow-up visit.

And he doubts that I have early-onset Alzheimer's! I'm so relieved. He thinks my worse-than-usual memory lapses are due to stress. Imagine that!

I took Ma to Benny Tudino's for lunch to prolong her outing. It was hard getting her and the walker out myself, but we managed. Every day there was a little less snow.

"He was such a nice man, Sibyl. Not like that one in Charleston who just wanted to use the knife. Cut, cut, cut. That's all some of these doctors want to do. I guess that's where the money is."

This was a familiar refrain, so I said my lines as if by agreement. "Some surgery really helps people, Ma. Remember my inflamed appendix? And Aunt Tootsie's bypass?"

She wasn't buying my argument any more than she ever had, so I was pleased when she reverted to the topic of Dr. De Cento. By the time our pizza came, she was saying, "Such gentle hands he had. I think your father should have a checkup with him too, don't you?"

Ma was still on good terms with Dad and Lenny. I prayed that eliminating her Valium would eliminate her confusion. Meanwhile, in between hiring lawyers, filling out medicare forms, and reading research papers, I ranted at Sol. "Since when don't you let me explain things to you? If we're supposed to be 'sharing our lives,' then why are you always away? How dare you think I'd put my own mother at risk? How could you jump to conclusions just because of somebody's appearance?" I went on and on, but he wasn't there to hear me. He didn't reply to my e-mail. I didn't know where to phone him. So now there were two of us at home talking to men who weren't there.

By Thursday of my spring break I was completely bonkers. That morning while I was taking a shower, Ma had wheeled into the bathroom and started talking to me about Sofia, the woman she'd met at the Grand Street Center. Even though Ma had done this before, I was caught off guard. I mean, there I was, naked under the streaming hot water trying to pull myself together after another night of weeping about my father and now Sol. That morning shower is a kind of transition time for me. When I heard her voice, I felt invaded and trapped. I lost it. I heard myself yelling at her, and I knew I had to get out of the house. I arranged for Pearl to spend the day with Ma.

I had planned to go to New York to a graduate-school seminar that evening, but I had some research of my own to do first. I spent the afternoon in the Jersey Room of the Jersey City Public Library. That third floor treasure trove holds material about New Jersey, painstakingly archived by the reference librarians. It's a major research center for those of us who take the Garden State seriously.

When I told the librarian what I wanted, he presented me with three fat folders of newspaper articles on Paulus Hook. Skimming the numerous articles detailing the history of this pre–Civil-War neighborhood named after a seventeenth-century Dutch settler, I focused instead on the pieces describing the controversy over routing the Bergen-Hudson Light Rail. I read some arguments in favor of the proposed route, including several letters to the editor from Jane Q. Public. I noted with interest that none of these was recent.

But the majority of letters and articles were negative. The residents of Essex Street, rowhouse and condo owners alike, all prophesied the doom of their neighborhood when this "monster" weighing 100 tons and measuring 100 feet in length ("the size of two blue whales") would zoom up and down their quiet residential street. According to these urban Cassandras, no other light rail system in the United States is so close to people's homes.

One reporter had interviewed a number of Essex Street homeowners who spoke anonymously. One man feared that when the serenity of the present street gave way to the sound of the speeding train, he would literally lose his mind. Another person focused on how the construction work would unsettle the local rats and release toxic fumes into the air. Still another, a preservationist, fantasized that the excavation would destroy artifacts from early American glass factories, iron works, and machine shops that once occupied that area. There was even a local African-American history buff who speculated that the pending construction would demolish a subterranean chamber that might have served as a stop on the Underground Railroad. Finally, the reporter told of a resident who claimed that the train would cause the value of her condo to plummet. She would lose her life savings. I Xeroxed the article.

By five, when I had to close the final folder and make my way back into the street, I had a hunch. On my way to the PATH train to New York, I detoured a few blocks to Paulus Hook. The cold evening air felt good. First I strolled up and down the segment of Essex Street where the train would pass, noting the impressive old row houses lining one side of the block and the brick condo facing them.

Then I walked over to Vinny's house on Sussex Street. It was a meticulously renovated classic Victorian brownstone. The stately manse, with its arched doorway and heavy, bracketed cornices, had an unobstructed view of some of the oldest surviving pre–Civil-War brick houses, not a speeding commuter train. There would always be a waiting list of yuppie tenants eager to pay high rents to occupy the former servants' quarters that Vinny had converted into a modish studio apartment.

As I stood on the sidewalk staring at the house, a familiar shadowy figure emerged from behind a parked car a few yards ahead of me. I did an abrupt about-face. I heard her footsteps moving faster behind me as I reached the corner. Determined to avoid Eleanor at all costs, I darted midblock into the rush-hour traffic on Grand Avenue, weaving between the infuriated drivers who honked in protest and braked just in time to miss me. It was a crazy thing to do, but it worked. Eleanor remained on the other side of the street long enough for me to join up with the many commuters coming from the Exchange Place PATH station. I resolved to get a restraining order.

Chapter 20

I wish you wouldn't fight the feelings you have for me. You could get hurt the way you run away. And another thing. Who was that new man who came to your house last week? I don't want him bothering you.

Professor Vallone is right. The bond that you and I share is very special. And like I said the last time, I will prove to you he said this.

Yours forever,
Eleanor

"I'm ready to get a restraining order on this woman," I said angrily. I threw Eleanor's latest missive on the table where Betty and Illuminada and I sat late Friday afternoon, slurping pea soup Betty had brought. I had found the note taped to the front door of my house the night before when I returned from my seminar. "I don't care if she is my student. She's really scary."

"Was there a flower or candy with this note?" asked Illuminada, picking up the piece of paper and scanning it. Before I could answer, she went on. "There does seem to be a threat here. Maybe two." She reread the note and handed it to Betty. "It's not so easy to get a restraining order on someone who's not related to you. But since we can demonstrate that she's been stalking you and we know she's got a history of mental illness . . ." Illuminada paused, considering the options.

Not to be left out, Betty spoke. "I've been reading up on erotomanics on-line. I have nothing better to do at night now." Occasional bitter asides like this one were the only expression Betty gave to her disappointment about no longer seeing Victor Vallone. "They can't form intimate relationships with others. They only have fantasy relationships like the one Eleanor has with you. If they can't maintain the fantasy, they can't survive. That's when they act out. So if you keep running away from Eleanor, she may act out. That could have been what happened with Vinny. It's kind of sad." Betty saw her own lovelorn state mirrored everywhere.

"What's sad, Betty, is that this woman is driving me nuts and may try to 'act out,' as you so charmingly put it, by bashing my head in. Or she may try to kill Sol." Even though I was pursuing the long-shot possibility of a murderer related to Vinny's alter ego as Jane Q. Public, Eleanor Chambers was still a primary suspect and my personal nemesis.

"Sol? Is he back? Why didn't you say so?" Betty asked.

I hated to explain, but I made myself say, "Sol's back from Prague, but he's not back here." I took a deep breath before going on. "He split."

There were a few seconds of silence, and then Betty fired off a series of questions. "What are you talking about, girl? Are you serious? When did he get home? What happened? Was it because of your mother?"

When I finished recapping the scene with Sol, I just sat there, tears welling, lip trembling. Betty and I were more or less in the same boat now, and it was sinking rapidly. Illuminada took pity on me first. "*Chiquita*, he'll come back. After you call him and apologize, he'll be back in a flash. Don't worry. He adores you. You just caught him off balance, that's all."

"I don't even know where he went. He doesn't answer my e-mail." I snuffled. "He didn't take anything. Just the luggage he came back with." When I heard myself mouth those words, I brightened a bit.

Betty must have been thinking the same thing, because she said, "Well, he'll have to return for his gear and then you both can talk and you can apologize and everything will be all right."

I decided not to pursue the "Bel will apologize" motif common to both their reconciliation scenarios. I'd have to think about that one. I thought we both had some apologizing to do. I blew my nose and said, "If we can tear ourselves away from the ruins of my love life for just a minute, I'd like to run a few things by you."

Betty put it in words first. "Yeah. Change the tape whenever you want. I'm ready."

Illuminada nodded, saying, "Sure. Go ahead."

"Remember your thing about leaving no stone unturned?" I was looking at Illuminada as I spoke. "Well, I learned that Vinny wrote several letters to the editor of the *Herald* using the pseudonym Jane Q. Public." In fact, Sarah had confirmed that Vinny and Jane Q. Public were one and the same within an hour of my call to her. "He wrote to support the routing of the light rail through Essex Street in Paulus Hook."

"Oh yeah. I read about that. That's causing quite a controversy." Illuminada looked thoughtful.

"Go on," said Betty.

"Well, Vinny's activism on behalf of that cause opens up a whole new area of his life that we didn't know about and haven't checked out. I mean we're looking at his students and at the family." I winced as I saw Betty's dark cheeks darken further at my reference to Victor Vallone. "And we're looking at the business too. So I think we should consider this angle as well. And . . ." I hesitated.

"*Dios mio*, Bel. There you go again. And *what*, for heaven's sake?"

"I love you when you're tearing your hair out with impatience, Illuminada. And I have an idea—a possible suspect. This one's a real reach, but . . . I think it'll be easy to verify this suspicion or put it away. All I need is a few free hours." By the time I had outlined my plan and they had, predictably, pronounced it mad, the dregs of our pea soup had caked on the bowls.

"Well, Betty, we owe you a birthday dinner. One of these days we'll come through." Monday had been Betty's birthday, and Illuminada and I had planned to take her to Casa Dante to cheer her up. But we had settled instead for late-afternoon soup at my house so I could stay home with Ma. I wondered how long it would be before I had a life again. Would I ever? As I said good-bye to my friends, I wallowed anew in self-pity.

And then I logged onto the *Jerusalem Post*.

SUICIDE BOMBING IN TEL AVIV

Three Killed and Many Wounded

At 1:45 P.M. a suicide bomber detonated a bomb shortly after sitting at a table on the terrace of the packed Apropo Cafe in Central Tel Aviv, where many families, including children still in Purim costumes, and tourists were gathered . . .

I sat frozen at the computer, literally paralyzed by fear. Shemayim, Mark's kibbutz, was a ten-minute ride from Tel Aviv, and he and his friends routinely headed there for R&R on their days off. I don't know how long I sat staring at the monitor, but when I heard Ma's walker and saw her petite frame silhouetted in the doorway, I realized it was way past time for dinner. I forced myself to reheat some leftover pot roast I had made the other night as part of my anti–chicken-breast campaign. I boiled water for noodles to go with the meat and unscrewed the top of a jar of applesauce.

"So what's the matter, Sibyl? You're not yourself."

What would she say if I said, "My son, your grandson, may be in smithereens as we speak. Daddy died. My lover has dumped me. I'm being stalked by a homicidal maniac, and, to top it all off, my mother, who has moved in with me, is driving me crazy"? I decided against this answer. Instead, I said simply, "Well Ma, there was another one of those bombings in Israel today, not far from where Mark is and I'm very worried about him."

My mother put down her fork and looked me in the eye, something she hadn't done in a long time. When she spoke I heard a vestige of the same soothing tone she once used to make her little girl believe that the orphaned Babar would manage somehow. But her message was straight Sadie Bickoff, inveterate gambler. "Sibyl, the odds are with him. He'll be fine. You'll see." Then she reached across the table, squeezed my hand, and said quite firmly, "Now eat this good dinner you made, before it gets cold." So I did.

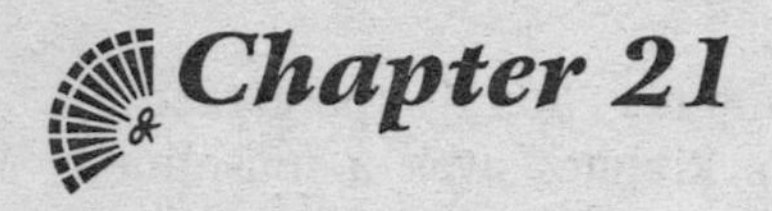

Chapter 21

How the Jehovah's Witnesses beliefs about Death Affect their Funerals

Joevelyn Tate
Funeral Service Education: Writing and Research
Professor Barrett
Draft 1
March 23, 1996

Introduction

I believe you can be a better funeral services director if you understand the beliefs the family of the diseased has about death and the life to come. My aunt has become a Jehovah's Witness and now she always telling us about her new religion. It is very different from my religion and there are a lot of people joining up with it now. I decided to do research on it to learn more about it for myself.

The Jehovah's Witnesses teach a doctrine known as Soul Sleep. Once the Soul Sleep period has passed and each individual has been judged, the ultimate destiny of all mankind is one of three options: Annihilation for most people; Paradise Earth for the majority of Jehovah's Witnesses; or Heaven, where a select 144,000 Witnesses will rule with Jesus. . . .

I don't think Joevelyn had meant to plagiarize, but it was clear as day that the second paragraph of her paper was lifted from an undocumented source. A quick glance at her "Works Cited" page revealed an unalphabetized and oddly formatted hodgepodge of articles, books, and websites. I'd have to go over the whole paper with her to review paraphrasing, quoting, and citing sources yet again. And we would work on proofreading beyond the spell check. It promised to be a long conference.

I began to write a response to her work that would, I hoped, be helpful and not discouraging. At least she hadn't downloaded a paper directly from a site—like schoolsucks.com—that sells research papers. Her plagiarism was unintentional and bore the same relationship to academic dishonesty that taking the wrong umbrella home from a party does to theft. It takes time and practice to learn the discourse and conventions of the academy well enough to churn out a good term paper. I knew Joevelyn had put a lot of effort into the research, so the next step would be teaching her how to cite from it and document it.

As I was scrawling my final suggestion, my head was filled with questions about the Witnesses. Joevelyn certainly had got me to thinking. Suddenly my brain did one of those leaps I've come to count on lately and, still musing on Joevelyn's findings, I realized how I could check out the residents of Essex Street.

Masquerading as a Jehovah's Witness was pretty

far-fetched, since my knowledge of that faith was based solely on what I had gleaned from Joevelyn's paper and my own brief encounters with Witnesses who had come to my door. I say "brief encounters" because I categorize all door-to-door solicitors as intruders. On the Bel Barrett Scale of Detestable Creatures, they rank a rung below even the vile telemarketers. The intrepid crusaders for the Witnesses always rang my doorbell when I was naked, on the phone, on the toilet, or in the middle of reading a student paper. It never failed. Needless to say, I was seldom patient with them. For my ploy to work, I was counting on my audience being more tolerant of the Witnesses than I was.

First I created a mock up of a *Watch Tower* cover with a block print headline screaming ARE YOU READY FOR THE DEATH OF SATAN? and a lot of fine print beneath it. The fine print was actually a handy Xerox of a recipe from the *New York Times* for vegetable lasagne. I glued my homemade cover over the latest issue of *Modern Maturity*, which looked to be about the size of the *Watch Tower*.

What does the well-dressed Witness wear? I took off my earrings and pulled an old navy blue ski cap of Sol's over my graying wild-woman hair. With a lipstick Rebecca had left last time she visited, I painted my mouth what turned out to be a brownish mauve. The black skirt and sweater I had on would do. I didn't intend to take off my parka. I was wearing flat-heeled boots, and I carried my huge kilim shoulder bag, presumably filled with copies of the *Watch Tower*. In this bag I stashed a black-and-crimson scarf, a pair of earrings featuring black stones set in rough chunks of silver, my camera, and a retractable tape measure. Slipping into my black (of course) parka, I was off.

I was lucky to find a parking space around the corner from Essex Street. After ringing the bell of the first town house I came to, I waited. It was Saturday, and somebody just might be home. Sure enough, I heard running footsteps, and then the massive carved door opened a crack. From somewhere within, the familiar voice of Kathy Smith counted and exhorted on an aerobics tape. The face of a scowling young woman, sweat dripping onto her yellow headband, poked out the door. Panting, she took one look at me standing there in my ski cap, clutching my pseudo *Watchtower* and flashing my brownish mauve smile, and slammed the door in my face. I guess I looked the part.

No one answered the door at the next house. But when I rang at the third house, I heard slow steps and, before long, the door swung open. I mentally crossed my fingers. "Hello. I'm Sister Betty Illuminada," I said, taking in the woman who faced me. She moved slowly and wore thick glasses. I'd say she was about eighty. She was bundled into a bulky blue and green sweater and gray slacks. "How would you like to live in a world free of crime and pollution? Do you know what lies ahead in the new world to come?"

"What lies ahead?" Her laugh was more like a sigh. "What lies ahead, my dear, is the light rail. It's going to lie right over there." She pointed out into the street. "Practically in my front garden." As she uttered the last phrase, her voice quavered a little.

I played dumb. "I'm sorry? What rail?" She backed a few steps into her vestibule to protect herself from the raw March wind. But she made no motion to close the door. In fact, she beckoned me to follow her into the shelter of the hallway. Like Ma, she was probably lonesome and glad for company.

"Haven't you heard? The Bergen-Hudson Light Rail is going to go right down this street. Millions of rodents will run through here once they start digging." She shuddered a little and hugged herself. "And talk about pollution. Poison gases will fume out of the ground. Place won't be fit to live in." This must be the woman who had expressed her concerns about health issues. She continued to talk, pleased to have a new forum for her dire predictions. "I've lived here all my life. I was raised right here in this house. My brother and I planted those trees there." She pointed in the general direction of three huge trees between the curb and the sidewalk in front of her house.

"It's a lovely home," I said, gazing with genuine admiration at the intricate carving atop the columns that flanked the door. "Do all your neighbors feel the same way about the train?" In an effort to get her to respond, I follwed my question immediately with "I bet the folks who live over there don't much care." I pointed at the ten-story condominium building across the street. "A train coming through here wouldn't bother them, up high as they are."

"Don't let Anna Haggardy hear you say that. She's on the first floor over there by the corner and she's fit to be tied. Put her life savings into her place, she did. A few of them on the lower floors who can afford to take a loss are leaving. Like the Harrises. They left, bag and baggage, last week. But not Anna Haggardy. She can't move, but she sure doesn't want to stay. You see . . ." My new conversational partner was just warming up, but by then I had what I came for and was eager to move on.

As politely as I could, I tried for closure. "In the

New World to come, there will be no rodents or poison fumes." With that promise, I stuck my makeshift pamphlet into the woman's hand, praying that she'd trash it without a second glance, unless, of course, she wanted a really good vegetable lasagne recipe. She had been so pleasant, I was tempted to tell her about it, but before I could give in to that impulse, I turned and left. Walking back to my car, I congratulated myself on the success of my ruse. Sister Betty Illuminada indeed! I couldn't wait to tell my two cohorts what a coup I had pulled off in their names.

Once I got to the car, I sat, not in the driver's seat but in the roomier passenger seat. There I began a makeshift makeover. I pulled off the ski cap and fluffed out my more-salt-than-pepper hair so it framed my face in wiry curls. I dug my black and silver earrings out of my bag and slipped the posts into my ears. Then I unfolded my crimson and black scarf and tied it loosely around my collar, tucking the ends into the front of my parka. Pulling down the mirror behind the sunshade, I checked the effect. The brownish mauve lipstick would have to go. I rubbed it off with a Kleenex, which left my lips just a bit reddened. I pinched my cheeks to give them a flash of color too. *Voila.* I was now a slightly ditsy real estate agent.

"Oh I'm so sorry. I can't seem to find the key to the Harris place. You don't mind if I just put this down here a minute, do you?" I was addressing the doorman of the Essex House Condominums and, before the startled young fellow had a chance to answer, I dumped the contents of my huge purse onto his desk, right there in the lobby. The camera and tape measure were clearly visible.

"Damn. I just can't imagine what I did with it. You know, come to think of it, I bet my granddaughter got into my purse again. She's at that age when they just love to play with keys, you know?" I looked up as I continued to rummage through the small mountain of personal belongings I carry around all the time. "I doubt if anybody will buy the Harris apartment now, but maybe I can get them a tenant willing to rent for a year. You know, until the construction starts."

I've never known a man comfortable in close proximity to the contents of a woman's purse. Sure enough, it wasn't long before the doorman, looking askance at the heap of stuff on his desk, offered, "Well ma'am, I can let you into the Harris place. I don't see no harm in that." He seemed very relieved when the last of my effects disappeared again into the maw of my kilim sack. Within a few minutes, we were inside the Harrises first-floor apartment.

I handed him a ten-dollar bill and said sweetly, "Thank you so much. You've been very kind. I'll just be about half an hour. I have to take some measurements and a few photos and write up an ad. I'll let myself out when I'm done. Now let me see. Where is that tape measure? I just saw it, so I know it's in here." While I spoke, I began rooting through my purse again.

Faced with the prospect of yet another outpouring from my bag, the doorman fled, saying quickly: "No problem. Just check with me when you leave the building, okay?" I waited until I was sure he was back at his post in the lobby before I left the Harris' condo and walked down the hall.

At the last door on the street side of the building, I paused for a moment and then rapped hard and pushed the buzzer at the same time. For the third time that morning, I heard steps. These were slow and accompanied by a rhythmic tapping sound, perhaps a cane. I imagined I saw an eye staring at me through the peephole. Then the door opened a couple of inches.

"Whuddya want?" The female voice that uttered these decidedly unwelcoming words was shrill and nasal.

As soon as I had sensed the eye at the peephole, I began to breathe quickly. Now I was gasping. "Oh. I'm so glad somebody's home. I'm looking for the Harris apartment, but I seem to be on the wrong floor or something. No one's answering." Then I teetered and grabbed onto the doorjamb for support. "Might I trouble you for a glass of water?" I was still breathing hard and doing a good imitation of a person about to faint. The door opened a little wider and the old woman, leaning on her cane, turned and hobbled slowly back into her living room. "Yeah." It was more of a snarl than an invitation, actually, but I'm not one to stand on ceremony. I collapsed into the nearest chair.

My reluctant hostess pulled a stained aqua dressing gown tightly around her and made her way slowly into the recessed kitchen. While she was running the tap, I checked out the apartment. The heavy curtains were drawn, so the room was dark even on a bright morning. Most of what light there was came from the TV screen, where two people sat discussing in graphic detail the sexual abuse one of them had suffered years ago at the hands of his Scout leader.

As Rebecca would say, the place was gross. Trust me, it really was. Piles of newspapers spilled into messy heaps on the floor. Even in the dim light I could see a thick film of dust coating every horizontal surface. And the musty air was redolent with the ammoniac attar of unchanged cat litter blended with just a hint of eau de canned cat food. At the thought of putting my lips to a glass from this apartment, I actually began to feel queasy.

But when the woman I assumed to be Anna Haggardy returned and unceremoniously stuck a glass of water in front of me, I took it and sipped dutifully before putting it on the table beside my chair. When I put the glass down, I noticed what I thought was a design carved in the surface of the tabletop. My nose wrinkled involuntarily when I saw that the "design" was, in reality, a circular depression in the layers of dust coating it. Trying not to gag, I placed my glass smack in its center, swearing to myself that as long as I breathed, my mother would never, ever live like this.

I spoke softly, as if it were a great effort. Years of conferencing with students had taught me that most everybody can be reached if you just keep at it. So I figured if I talked long enough, I'd push the right button and say something that would make this surly old lady open up. "Thank you so much. I still feel a little woozy. I haven't had one of these spells in months. But I'm sure I'll be all right in a minute or two. Then, if you'll let me use your phone, I'll call my nephew. I so wanted to surprise him. That's why I told the doorman a tiny fib to get up here without buzzing them. . . ." I was rewarded when Anna Haggardy reacted almost violently to the word *doorman*.

"The doorman? That wise-ass punk's not worth the space he takes up. He don't keep nobody out. Half the time he's down by the corner talking to some little slut instead of in front of the building where he belongs." Her voice was gruff, and her eyes burned with a rage too great to be accounted for by a slacker doorman. "You can't get decent people to work for you today, even if you're willing to pay top dollar." Anna Haggardy shrugged. I nodded.

When she continued, her words came out in a sustained growl. "Take the bimbo my dumb son got in here to clean this place—somebody he met in that dumb job he got." Anna Haggardy shrugged again. "She didn't do nothin' but break stuff and lie about it. I mean that lazy little bitch never even moved a piece of furniture or bent down to scrub a baseboard. And she broke the vacuum that I had since my first husband." Women who bad-mouth the people they pay to clean their homes are a pet peeve of mine, right up there with door-to-door canvassers and telemarketers. I mean, if somebody doesn't work well, find someone else or do the work yourself. But spare me that song and dance about the unmoved furniture and the damn baseboards.

I said, "You're so right. It is hard to get good help today."

Anna Haggardy, encouraged by my feigned agreement, continued. "I let her come only twice. Do you know what that lying bitch did? She broke my one good piece. A marble bust that my first husband bought me. Looked just like me, he said." Was her voice softening just a little? I was prepared to share an elegaic and nostalgic moment when she went on. "He took off two weeks after he give it to me, the bastard. But I kept it right there. As a reminder." A bony arthritic finger pointed to my water glass. "And that clumsy pig must've knocked it over. She denied it, the lying slut. Afraid I'd make her pay for it probably. But I know she broke it. Took the pieces home in her bag. I know it sure as I'm sittin' here."

Anna Haggardy had lowered herself slowly into the chair in front of the TV while she was talking. "It must be hard to lose something so precious," I said in what I hoped was a sympathetic tone.

"You think that's bad?" Now she was actually sputtering, a thin spray of spittle accompanying her tirade. "See this place?" She waved an arm, taking in the entire dirt museum with this gesture. "When my dumb son heard about this place and told me to buy it for my retirement, I thought he had a really hot tip. What a moron. I put every penny I had into it. And for what?" She paused a moment. I hoped my face wore a puzzled look. I wanted her to continue.

When she did, it seemed as if she were changing the subject. "You ain't gonna find the Harrises here. If you'd a spoke to the doorman, you'd know. They moved. They had the money, so they got out before—" I adjusted my expression to reflect surprise at this information.

"Oh no! I haven't seen my nephew in years. So I had no idea. His mother, my sister, she passed on several years ago. We've been out of touch." I was heavily into damage control now, trying to reweave the fragile web of my masquerade. "Why would he want to leave here? It's such a lovely neighborhood, such a solid building." I pressed on, hoping her need to vent would be greater than her suspicion of my story.

"We all want to leave here now. Look." Slowly, leaning heavily on her cane, Anna Haggardy heaved herself out of her chair. She shambled over to the front window and dramatically pulled the curtain. I was briefly blinded by the late winter sunlight that streamed suddenly into the room. This was a good thing because it kept me from rising too quickly. I didn't want to arouse her suspicions before she had told me the rest of her story.

Shielding my face from the sun with my hands, I walked carefully over to where she stood. "Look at that," she repeated. I looked. What I saw was a familiar-looking blue Toyota Corolla wagon parallel parking across the street. For a moment my heart stopped. Mark drove a car just like that. I never recognize cars, but I had driven a royal blue Toyota Corolla wagon identical to that for five years before giving it to Mark. A familiar-looking figure was getting out and unloading two grocery bags. But it wasn't Mark. It was Arthur Hoffman. Of course. He probably lived on Essex Street. That would account for the impassioned speech he'd made decrying the coming of the light rail to this block.

Anna Haggardy's voice was now a low rumble. "Look. See that spot over there? Where that blue station wagon just parked? Not fifteen feet from here? They're goin' to run a goddamn train through there. And now my place ain't worth shit." These last words were a harsh whisper and once she had said them, Anna Haggardy let the curtain fall, plunging the room once again into semidarkness before I could respond. As my eyes adjusted to the reduced light, I heard a key turning in the lock.

I must have tensed because Anna Haggardy said, "Oh don't worry, that's just my jackass son." Arthur Hoffman shuffled into the room lugging two bags of groceries. Arthur lived here? In this sty? "Haggardy the Horrible" was his mother? I couldn't believe it. But I was not the only one who was surprised. When Arthur saw me, his eyes widened. His initial smile of greeting didn't last long.

"P . . . P . . . P . . . Professor Barrett! Wh . . . Wh . . . What are you doing here?" Arthur stammered. His eyes were lowered and his head hung. There was no trace of the confident young activist who'd addressed the CCPW meeting just a few weeks ago. I prayed that nothing Arthur said would contradict my cover story. Damn! What a time for a former student to show up. I talked fast.

"Arthur. What a nice surprise. I'm just trying to track down a relative who used to live in this building, and I felt a bit ill. Your mom gave me some water." I pointed at the water glass on the filthy tabletop. "But what are you doing here?" With my rhetorical question, I hoped to distract him from thinking too hard about what I had just said.

"Be all day before that mumble-mouthed jackass answers you. You got all day?" Now I was literally speechless with horror. Anna Haggardy was relentless. "That big moron there is the rocket scientist who heard about this place and told me to buy it. You professors didn't teach him nothing at that college." With a groan of disgust, she lowered herself into her chair again and barked at Arthur: "What are you just standing there for? Put them groceries away before they rot. What time you got to be at work today?"

"T . . . T . . . Two," stuttered Arthur, misery rendering his voice nearly inaudible, as he lumbered toward the kitchen with a bag in each hand. I couldn't stand seeing him like this, witnessing his mother shame him, watching him cower. It was obscene.

"Thank you so much for the water. I'm feeling better now. Good-bye. Good-bye Arthur," I said as I stood, buttoned my parka, and let myself out. Alone in the elevator, I felt shaky. What series of events had turned Arthur's mother into a monster—a monster who fed on her own young?

Chapter 22

MIDNIGHT GRAVE DIGGER
TRIES TO WAKE THE DEAD

Responding to a call from an area resident walking his dog, police entered St. Anselmo's Cemetery in Jersey City late last night and arrested a woman digging at a gravesite there. Thirty-two-year-old Eleanor Chambers of Jersey City, a student in the Funeral Services Education Program at River Edge Community College, had dug through the snow and was attempting to penetrate the frozen ground when police arrested her at the grave of Vincent Vallone Jr., of Vallone and Sons Funeral Home. Vallone had been her instructor at the College. Chambers told police: "I'm digging up his grave to show that he's not in it. Because he's still alive." Chambers, an employee of Floral Tribute, Inc., on West Side Avenue, is being held at Saint Francis Hospital pending a psychiatric examination.

"Get your lazy butt out of bed, girlfriend, and look in the paper. Page three. Upper right." It was Betty's voice on the phone, bright and early on Wednesday morning. When I had read the article, I exhaled slowly. I could feel my neck muscles relax. I called Betty right back.

"Thank God. I'm so glad that poor woman is off the streets. My street especially." I was also relieved not to have to worry about getting a restraining order on her myself.

"Yeah. Maybe it's time to go to the cops about her. Now that we know she's got a record and she's clearly nuts, I think they'll be willing to at least consider that she might have killed Vinny." For a moment I regretted having done such a good job of convincing Betty that Eleanor was a plausible suspect. Betty's eagerness to close the case was probably fueled at least as much by her desire to vindicate Victor Vallone as it was by her zeal to see justice done. She wasn't going to take kindly to new input at this point. I plunged ahead anyway.

"Let's talk before we do anything drastic. Remember, I was looking into the CCPW angle?" I kept my voice light, hiding the mix of excitement and apprehension I felt.

"You know what your problem is, Bel?" Betty sounded put out. She was so miserable lately that she often sounded that way. Being in love had agreed with her. It used to agree with me too. But I wasn't going to think about Sol anymore. Thinking about him just made me miserable too. He hadn't returned my phone calls to his cell phone or my e-mail.

"No, tell me." I'd humor her. Why not?

"You can't do anything without talking about it first. But you're probably right. I'll call Illuminada. Which is better for you, tonight or tomorrow?" I had to hand it to Betty. She was really trying.

The next night worked out better for all of us. Ma had gone to bed especially early because she was going on a day trip with Pearl on Friday to Atlantic City, of all places. This was another one of Pearl's brainstorms. As soon as she heard that Ma hadn't been to Atlantic City since before it had become a casino capital, Pearl got after me to let her take Ma on one of those bus trips for seniors. Now that the roads were no longer paths in the snow, I had agreed. Ma was really up for it. We had laid out a mustard-colored knit pants suit and a scarf with a design of flame red and gold. When I kissed her good night, Ma whispered for the tenth time, "Twenty five bucks is my limit, Bel. I swear." That's what Ma was saying. Sadie Bickoff was another story. At least she was saying it to me, not to my dad or to Lenny. Maybe, just maybe, taking her off Valium was helping.

I was too tired from a day of conferences and committee meetings to cook, so I called Illuminada and asked her to pick up some eggplant parmigiana and pasta from Lisa's on the way over. I had a bottle of Soave, Marie's bread, and fresh greens.

Illuminada looked up as she poured oil on her salad. "I know you've got something on your mind, Bel. So tell us before you burst. What happened when you went to Essex Street?"

"Well you know I had this student whose aunt became a Jehovah's Witness," I began.

"*Caramba* Bel! Before you even start, give us the abridged version, please." It was Illuminada of course, bugging me to get to the point before I even hit my stride. But by the time I finished telling them about my stint as a Jehovah's Witness, we were all giggling and the bottle of Soave was emptying fast.

"Now did I ever tell you about this student I had

in Speech last semester who—," Betty and Illuminada groaned in unison. "No. I mean, seriously. Listen." They resigned themselves to another narrative outburst on my part. When I explained how I got by the doorman, I saw Illuminada take out her notebook and jot something down. Maybe she wanted to remember the ruse of the overflowing purse to use herself someday. When I described the grunge pit Anna Haggardy called home, Betty stuck her finger down her throat, so I knew she was paying attention. And finally, when I recounted Arthur's arrival and told how his mother belittled him in front of me, their faces mirrored my own horror.

"So you're saying this crippled old woman killed Vinny because he wrote a letter to the editor in favor of the train going down her street?" Betty looked dubious even as she framed her question.

"How could a woman in her eighties who can't even walk without a cane manage to hit Vinny Vallone so hard he died from the blow and then, how would she dump him in the river? Not." Illuminada wasn't buying this theory either.

"Wait. There's more." I stacked our empty plates and carried them into the kitchen. "Today I was followed again." I called this over my shoulder from the sink where I was running hot water over the plates, so the cheese would be easier to get off later on. "Wait a minute." I quickly put on a pot of decaf and grabbed a box of biscotti.

I returned to the dining-room table, carrying the biscotti. Betty looked at it and cracked, "Well, here I was thinking you were in the kitchen having a Julia Child moment, Bel." When I smiled, she asked, "Did you just say you were followed today? How can that be? Eleanor is in a padded room at Saint Francis, praise the Lord."

"I know, but I was on the stairwell at school this afternoon and there were footsteps behind me. Whenever I stopped, the footsteps stopped. I didn't wait around to see who it was. When I got to the third floor, I took the elevator. But I'm sure there was somebody there. And . . ." I hesitated.

"And? And what, Bel?" Illuminada was returning from the kitchen with the coffee pot and a mug of hot water for my tea. I hadn't even heard the microwave signal. "Maybe the little bit of caffeine in this will speed you up," Illuminada said, putting the mug in front of me.

"And there was a blue Toyota Corolla wagon parked around the corner from here when I got home from work." Before considering the import of this announcement, we all dunked our chocolate biscotti in our hot drinks. Then, for once unbidden, I continued slowly. "I really hate to say this, but I think Arthur Hoffman killed Vinny Vallone. And, I think he may very well try to kill anybody else he thinks is pushing for the light rail to take the Essex Street route."

"*Como mierda*! You think that pathetic kid did it? The stutterer? Why? How? Remember motive, method, and opportunity, Bel." I noted that Illuminada was not dismissing my idea now, but rather honoring it with questions.

"As for why, I think he's crazy. Not crazy like Eleanor or even"—here I blinked a little—"like my mother, but crazy like you get when somebody belittles and shames you all your life. I think his mother is the reason he stutters, and she is also the root of the reason he killed. And may kill again. In fact, he may already have killed other people."

"I buy that his mother has made him crazy even though I hate to blame a mother. Blaming Mom is so old," Betty said wearily. "It's always our fault, right? But what would he hope to accomplish by killing Vinny?" Betty had a point. It was a crucial one too.

"He accepts what his mother tells him and blames himself for the fact that she bought a condo on Essex Street with her life savings. And that condo is his inheritance. So now he's trying to stave off the train. I guess he figures if he can cause such a big problem, he can solve it."

Betty looked up then. "Is this the first you noticed something was wrong with him?"

"Well, frankly, I thought he was sort of a savant type. You know he drew incredibly complex diagrams for several of his speeches. But as his Speech teacher, I focused on his shyness and his stutter. And I just kept patting myself on the back for the great job I did teaching him public speaking in spite of his disability. If it hadn't been for hearing him speak at the CCPW meeting and then recognizing Vinny's writing style in that letter to the editor, I never would have associated the two of them." I paused and helped myself to another biscotti. "Although now that I think of it, Arthur was at Vinny's viewing."

"So you figure he just overpowered Vinny and conked him on the head and threw the body in the canal?" Betty queried.

"Basically that's exactly what I think. I even have a pretty good idea of what the murder weapon was, but I don't think we'll ever find it," I said slowly.

"*Dios mio!* What do we have to do to get you to share with us what you think the murder weapon was?" asked Illuminada, crossing her arms in front of her and tilting her head.

So I told them about the water glass and the dust ring on the tabletop and the marble bust of a woman that Anna Haggardy's first husband had given her. Before I finished, Illuminada was nodding. "I think he got Vinny to agree to get together with him somewhere on some pretext or other, and then bashed Vinny's head in with the bust and dumped him and the sculpture in the water. Arthur is a great hulk of a young man and Vinny probably suspected nothing. Arthur wouldn't have had any difficulty with the bashing or the dumping."

"Do you think his mother put him up to it?" Betty was still prodding.

"No. I don't. I don't think she thinks he's capable of anything so . . ." Now I was stammering, at a loss for a word to describe what I believed Arthur had done.

"*Macho*? Is that what you mean?" Illuminada was half right.

"Yes. And aggressive. Killing Vinny won't stop the light rail. It wasn't a very bright thing to do, but it was certainly aggressive. And she thinks he's too dumb and scared to do squat, let alone plan and carry out a murder." I sighed, picturing Anna Haggardy's sour expression and hearing again her words "my dumb son."

"Well, Bel, now we have more questions than answers." Illuminada was thinking out loud. "We need to know how this supposedly learning-disabled *hombre* figured out that Jane Q. Public really was Vinny, and then how he connected with him and disposed of his body without being noticed. All we have is a suspicion of a motive. Henry, Eleanor, Gilberto, and even Victor also had motives." Illuminada glanced at Betty as she ended her list of suspects with Victor's name.

"Give me a few more days. I've got a couple of ideas."

Chapter 23

March 27, 1996

Dear Bel,

I guess your pathological envy has kept you from writing. I wouldn't dream of rubbing your nose in it, but being on sabbatical is just so liberating and intellectually intense. It's lovely to be here on Beatrix Potter's home turf in the Lake District, especially off season. I've been reading and writing in the mornings and visiting the local Potter shrines in the afternoons. I try to get back to my B&B in time for tea and homemade scones dripping with jam and clotted cream, but what do you care about that, right?

In another week I head to London to check out Beatrix's childhood home and use the library there. The poor woman's life is filled with textbook examples of prefeminist problems. Would you believe her parents wouldn't allow her to marry because they wanted her to take care of them in their old age? I may actually come up with an article. I love teaching Chil-

dren's Lit at RECC, but the life of a vagabond scholar has its rewards too.

Do write and catch me up on all the news. How's life in the death department? Relax, I'm sure Mark is fine. Try not to hate me. Don't forget to water Thelma and Louise.

Love,
Wendy

Although I didn't hate Wendy, I sure wouldn't have minded changing places with her. But RECC grants only one sabbatical leave a year and Wendy was the lucky one this year. If I ever had time to answer her letter, where would I start? With Vinny's murder? Rebecca's accident? My dad's death? Or how about with my mother's problems? On the other hand, maybe Sol's defection would make a zingy opener. Wendy would be appalled when she heard about Eleanor Chambers stalking me.

I was now pretty sure that Eleanor was no longer part of the problem. In fact, I'd figured out how she might actually be part of the solution. I reasoned that since she'd followed Vinny around the way she'd followed me, she probably knew something that might help us. As Mark would say, "Duh." So I had decided to talk to her. After weeks of avoiding Eleanor, I was actually going to seek her out at St. Francis and see if I could get her to tell me anything of interest she might have noticed about Vinny's last days, like what happened to him after he left work on the day he was killed, for starters.

"Excuse me? No, Bel. You're not going to visit Eleanor Chambers in the psych ward and grill her. No way." Illuminada laid this on me in her Threat Management Specialist voice during a late-night telephone conversation. "She's probably taking her meds now, and maybe she's behaving better, but you never know when she'll go off again. They won't keep her there for long, trust me. Even though you don't think she killed Vinny, you don't want to give her any fuel for future delusions. You are not to make contact with her under any circumstances. Am I making myself clear?"

"Yes ma'am. So how—"

"Save your breath, *chiquita*. I'll go talk to her." She sounded resigned, but I didn't care. It was important that we learn whatever Eleanor could tell us. "I'll stop by your office later today and tell you how I make out. I know a few people at St. Francis, so getting access to her shouldn't be a problem. I just hope she's feeling chatty. Now may I go back to sleep?"

The next afternoon I was in my office typing up the minutes of our last department meeting, a chore that rotated alphabetically to people who didn't have the sense to come late to the meeting when it was their turn. I had left the office door open because it was stuffy inside. We either had no heat or we suffocated. Illuminada knocked on the open door. When she shut it firmly behind her, I knew she had something substantive to report. Just as she began taking off her coat and settling into Wendy's chair, the phone rang. I reached for it. "Professor Barrett," I said automatically.

"Sibyl? Sibyl, is that you dear?"

This was a new development. Ma had not called me at school. In fact, she hadn't been working the phone at all. Pearl called if there was a problem or she wanted to know where something was. What could be wrong? Had something happened to Pearl?

I was painfully aware of how completely dependent we'd become on Pearl. What if she'd had a stroke? What if . . .

"Sibyl?" Ma sounded impatient, but not hysterical. Her voice was strong.

"Yes, Ma. It's me. Is anything wrong?" I crossed my fingers and shrugged my shoulders at Illuminada, whose face had screwed into a question mark.

"No. Pearl wanted to leave you a note, but I thought we'd call. We're going to the Grand Street Center now for a program and won't be back until around dinner time. But don't worry. If Henry can't pick us up, we'll take a cab home." A vivid sense of déjà vu flooded my brain. I'd had this conversation with Ma a thousand times when I was a teenager. I used to call her at work to tell her of a change in after-school plans. Oh God. I would think about this later.

"Sounds great, Ma. Have a good time." My hand trembled a little as I put down the phone and turned to face Illuminada.

"Everything okay in the motherland?" Illuminada inquired playfully.

"Yeah. She's using the phone again. She's letting me know she's going to the Center with Pearl. She sounds good, less confused, more in the present, and yet . . ." I held my hands up to signify that I wanted to table the conversation. I wasn't up to discussing role reversal right now.

"Okay, okay." Illuminada took a pear from her purse and offered me a bite. I shook my head and indicated my thermos of tea on the desk. "They let me talk to Eleanor for a few minutes. They got her back on her meds, which they said help her a lot. If she would just take the meds . . ." Illuminada paused, shaking her head. "Anyway, she looks sort of washed out and very anxious. Her nails are all chewed down, even the cuticles. She was folding and unfolding a Kleenex the whole time we talked. And she kept rubbing her fist in one eye. She seems a lot younger than she is. . . ."

I flashed back to the childlike Eleanor, retracting her head into her scarf, and nodded. Now that she was institutionalized, I felt free to sympathize with her once again. But my mental tape rewound and I recalled the weird notes and messages, the roses and M&M's, and that truly abominable snowman. These had been really scary. Eleanor was really scary. I was glad Illuminada had talked me out of going to see her myself.

Illuminada said quickly, "I told her the truth, that I was a PI investigating the death of Professor Vallone and that I knew she'd been 'keeping track' of his whereabouts pretty closcly."

"She sure was 'keeping track,' " I interjected. "What a delicate way of saying 'stalking.' Did they teach you that kind of tact in PI school?" I could seldom resist ribbing Illuminada just a little.

She gave me a dirty look over the remains of her pear and, feinting, aimed the core straight at my head before tossing it into the wastebasket. "So she thinks for maybe two seconds and she says, 'DGB four four one six.' " My face must have reflected my bewilderment, because Illuminada interrupted her narrative to look at me pityingly, "It's the license plate, stupid. Think about it. If you're going to follow people all over, it helps to memorize license numbers. Anyway, I checked it out before I came over here, and it is the license plate of one Arthur Hoffman." Illuminada grinned the way she does when she tells how she has wormed a particularly rewarding piece of information out of somebody. "And, Eleanor also said that Arthur Hoffman gave Vinny a ride home occasionally because they both lived in the same neighborhood."

"Good work! So now we can prove that Vinny knew Arthur. They probably met when Vinny brought stuff in to be copied, maybe even one of his Jane Q. Public letters. Arthur didn't even have to make the connection. He knew exactly who had brought the letter in. And better yet, now we also know that the two men had been together shortly before Vinny was killed." I was very excited.

Illuminada gave me a withering look. "*Dios mio*, Bel. Not so fast. Think about it. Eleanor is a certified nutcase who would not be considered a reliable witness by anyone but you."

"Of course. You're right. But I have a pretty good idea of where to find some hard evidence. Trust me."

Illuminada rolled her eyes as she gathered up her coat and briefcase and turned to go. I was already working out the details of my scheme.

Later that day, after I finished commenting on the last of a set of speech outlines, I was getting ready to leave the office, when there was another knock on the door. This time it was Henry Granger. "Yo, Professor Barrett." He was in the office before I had even swiveled my chair around. I was ashamed of the clutch I felt in my chest as I heard the door close behind him. We hadn't talked outside of class since the day Henry had been a principal player in the slapstick scene that had ended the only decent relationship of my adult life.

"What can I do for you, Henry?" I queried, gesturing for him to sit down in Wendy's chair. Instead he leaned against her desk, and looked down at me in my chair. I broke out in a sweat, one of those retro hot flashes that I still get every now and then just for old time's sake.

When Henry spoke, his voice was low and lazy, just a murmur really. "The police. They came by my house again last night. My grandmother, she don't know. She at church. They still ain't got no other suspects, and they act like they gettin' close to takin' me in." A vein on his neck pulsed rapidly, in sharp contrast to the soft slowness of his words.

"Henry, I'm working on an idea. But I need some help from you. What do you know about breaking into cars?" I said purposefully.

"Why you askin', Professor? You gettin' ready to do a jack?" A rare grin inched its way across Henry's face. When he smiled, his tattoos were hardly noticeable.

Chapter 24

CCPW Hosts Reception
to celebrate
Groundbreaking
for Bergen-Hudson Light Rail
7:30 Friday evening, March 29
Hoboken City Hall
Slide show narrated by Sol Hecht,
Waterfront Historian and Preservationist

Wine and Cheese!
Come and party or come and help.
Volunteers call Marlene Proleteriat
at 201-555-9872

I barely had time to congratulate myself on the simple elegance of my plan when I read the notice from the Citizens' Committee to Preserve the Waterfront that awaited me in the day's mail. My hands turned to ice. Jesus. Sol would speak, and when poor, demented Arthur Hoffman heard Sol wax ecstatic over the routing of the light rail through Paulus Hook and on the west side of Hoboken. . . . Who knows? Arthur might very well take it into his head to try to silence Sol. Permanently.

Sol's one-man road show was dynamite. It was what had ultimately convinced the governor to back the light rail project. Sol's slides and accompanying statistics were more powerful than anything Jane Q. Public (aka Vinny Vallone) had ever written in a letter to the editor. If he heard Sol, poor Arthur would most certainly be set off. I had to warn Sol.

The reception was the next night, so I asked Pearl to stay late and keep Ma company. The problem was, Sol hadn't returned my calls or my e-mail. I'd have to go to city hall myself and try to get him out of there before his slide show. What would I say to him? "Sol, forget about you and me for now. This is not about us. It's about someone trying to kill you if you speak tonight. Just get out of here. I'll explain as soon as we leave." He'd have to pay attention. I could leave with him and we could sit down and talk over a glass of wine. And then, who knows? As Marlene Proletariat always says, the first time Sol and I left a CCPW meeting together, we . . . well, that was another time. However, I did dress carefully in the black cashmere pullover Sol had given me last Chanukah, my long black skirt, and his favorite earrings, the tigereye and macrame ones.

Hoboken's city hall is a popular setting for officially sanctioned parties. The landmark building has enough interior marble and wrought iron to make paying a parking ticket feel like a ceremonial rite. I sometimes picture Rebecca being married there. She would float down the central staircase in a cloud of white organdy, but that's another story. It was a real coup for CCPW to be in such good graces with the municipal power structure that we could actually host an event in city hall.

At the cocktail hour that preceded Sol's talk, I recognized the mayors of not only Hoboken and Jersey City, but also Bayonne and Weehawken. There were several local pols and a lot of folks on city payrolls milling around. Where was Sol? Just as I was about to impale a chunk of supermarket cheddar on a toothpick, I caught a glimpse of Marlene Proletariat.

Did she look unusually animated, or was that my imagination? Her normally severe expression was softened by a smile and that twitch of her facial muscles accented a dimple I'd never noticed before. Instead of her usual jeans and CCPW sweatshirt, Marlene wore a soft rose sweater over a pair of black leggings. I'd never noticed how thin she was.

I wouldn't dream of wearing leggings myself. When I tried on a pair of Rebecca's once, I flashed back to when I was a little girl teetering around in Sadie's black-patent leather high heels. The sophisticated, too-big shoes had contrasted sharply with my prepubescent torso and baby face. Sheathed in Rebecca's leggings, my still girlish legs below a forgiving tunic contrasted sharply with the laugh-lined face and graying hair above. I looked like a midlife mama in her daughter's leggings. It was not a fashion statement I cared to make.

But barely into her forties, Marlene looked even younger and extremely attractive. I was about to go over and ask her if she knew where Sol was, when my stomach tightened. Sol was approaching Marlene familiarly, holding a glass of wine in each hand. Instantly I understood Marlene's metamorphosis. Had she been harboring him in her Hoboken ceramics studio since he'd stormed out of my life? Were she and

Sol actually sleeping together? At the thought of these two ardent environmentalists sharing blissed-out post-coital discussions of waterfront development, I felt sick.

Before I could flee the party, I remembered why I was there. I had to save Sol. Oh my God. It was too late.

The lights dimmed, and there was a scraping sound as people pulled chairs from the perimeter of the room to the area in front of the screen. Marlene introduced the mayors. Then, in a husky, unfamiliar voice, she said a few glowing words about Sol. He approached the front of the room to a round of applause and I heard his rich bass begin.

"The riverbank is our legacy to . . ." The tears in my eyes prevented them from adjusting immediately to the darkness. Sol was pointing to a slide of a sleek train and saying, "Twenty-seven thousand commuters will travel each day up and down the Bergen-Hudson corridor, decreasing car travel and its attendant air pollution and traffic jams . . ."

I spotted Arthur Hoffman's now familiar bulk positioned directly across the room from Sol. Sol hadn't noticed me and neither had Arthur. So far so good. I kept my head down by pretending to take notes. When Sol finally finished speaking and had taken the requisite number of questions from the enthusiastic audience, people began to leave. I stayed in the background near the darkened city clerk's office just around the corner from the stairwell leading to the door. When I saw Sol help Marlene into a chic black leather coat (where was that ratty army jacket she had always worn?) and head for the door, I waited. Sure enough, Arthur left right behind them. I followed him.

Sol and Marlene were not holding hands, but was

that because he held his briefcase with his precious slides in one hand? Yes. He stopped a moment and put the entire briefcase into his backpack, freeing his hands. Marlene took his arm. They went on, heading for the PATH station a few blocks away. Were they going into New York? Was Sol taking Marlene to Chez Michallet, his favorite Village restaurant, to splurge on a romantic celebratory meal? I hoped my tears wouldn't prevent me from keeping all three of them in my line of vision.

To my surprise, Sol and Marlene continued past the train station. Oh my God! They were headed for the ferry. The Port Authority subway trains, New Jersey Transit railway trains and the ferry to the financial district all came and went under the same copper-turned-green roof of Hoboken's old Erie Lackawanna terminal.

Oh no! Sol was going to take Marlene by ferry to the riverfront walkway at the World Financial Center. It would be deserted there at this hour on a March night. But Sol didn't know there was any danger. Would they stop at the marina so he could read her the lines from Whitman on the wall there in the moonlight? Arm in arm they'd stroll the length of the promenade, pausing occasionally to . . . The rhythmic lapping of the river against the aged wooden piers interrupted my thoughts.

As they approached the ticket booth, I saw a ferry waiting at the slip. There were only a few other passengers boarding. Sol and Marlene must have noticed the boat too, for they began to walk faster. Sol plunked down money for their tickets, and they ran toward the boat. Their footsteps echoed in the near empty stone building. As Arthur, trotting now, approached the ticket booth, I heard my voice shriek,

"Arthur! Arthur! Is that you?" Arthur stopped in his tracks, like the proverbial startled deer.

His eyes glowed and he was breathing hard. "Professor Barrett?" He was momentarily too surprised to stutter, I noted. I could see him trying to puzzle out why I kept turning up, first at his home and now here. I had run to catch up with him, so I was out of breath too. But I didn't care. Out of the corner of my eye, I saw the ferry pull away. Sol was safe! I was enormously relieved.

My relief was shortlived, however. The ticket booth slammed shut. That must have been the last ferry of the evening. Now I was alone in the darkness of the deserted ferry landing with a murderer. "Arthur, I just wanted to . . ."

"Y . . . Y . . . Y . . . you following me? Wh . . . Wh . . . Why do you keep following me?" Arthur may stutter, but he is far from brain-dead, no matter what his mother thinks. And he did not know of my relationship with Sol, so his guilt-driven conclusion that I was following him again was logical.

"Oh Arthur. I'm so sorry. Now you've missed your boat, and it's all my fault." I hoped that by ignoring his question and taking a few steps back in the direction of the railroad's waiting room I'd distract him. In the railway terminal itself there would be at least a conductor or two and a few late commuters waiting for their train. I would have given anything to see the hordes of dressed-for-success commuters who charged the ferry landing during morning rush hour. But Arthur didn't move toward the terminal. Instead he grabbed my arm and pulled me back into the dark corridor leading to the boat landing, where black waves slapped the pilings.

"Yo, Professor Barrett! Sorry I'm late. I had me

some urgent business to take care of. Sorry to keep you waitin' here. This ain't no place to be by yourself. Never know what kinda trash 'n' whatnot you find here." Henry Granger had materialized out of the shadows near the closed ticket booth.

As soon as he saw Henry, Arthur dropped my arm as if it were a live fuse. Henry held one hand in his jacket pocket and with the other he took my arm. "This dude ain't bother'n you none now, is he?" The deceptively mellow way Henry slowly hissed these words was utterly menacing. Arthur's eyes darted from Henry's tattoos to the hand Henry kept in his pocket. I realized that Arthur thought Henry was pointing a gun at him. Bug-eyed, Arthur took a few steps backward and then turned and broke into an awkward run. He never looked over his shoulder.

I was too shaky to say anything as Henry and I walked through the station and back to his car, still double-parked across the street from city hall. Henry, however, talked a mile a minute. "Yestiday when you was talkin' about breakin' into a car, I figure you closin' in on somebody. Then when my grandmother told me she workin' late tonight so you could go out, I decided I just come along after you. My grandmother, she say your mother say sometime you got more heart than head, and you know what? She right. You a smart lady. Know all about citin' sources and makin' speeches and Standard English grammar and research and whatnot, but that ain't gonna help you none when you up against a killer. I don't mean no disrespect, Professor, but you ain't got no business goin' after no killer by yourself. I never 'spected you to do that. I just figured you scope out who smoked Professor Vallone, and let the cops take it from there. Sheeeeit."

Henry let out his breath in a long sigh of exasperation. But he wasn't done yet. "And your man. He got hisself a new woman. You got no call to be puttin' yourself out on his account." At any moment I expected Henry to stop the car, wag his index finger in my face, and say, "Naughty! Naughty!"

"Henry, you're right." As he double-parked in front of my house, I continued wearily: "I guess I really have to act fast now. I'll get the car business over with tomorrow night as planned." When Henry nodded, I said, "And, Henry, thank you for being there tonight. I'm not much of a swimmer." When my feeble joke failed to elicit even a smile from him, I said, "I'll tell your grandmother you're here to drive her home. She'll be right out."

Chapter 25

To: Caregivers@senior.net
From: Bbarrett@circle.com
Re: The Condo
Date: 04/02/96 06:08:44

Thanks, John, Yvette, and Sharon for your warning that I not go to Charleston to empty my parents' apartment with only my mother because we'll be too depressed. But we really don't have anyone else to go with us. My daughter's in school in Seattle. My son is in Israel. All my friends work. And my "life partner" has dumped me and taken up with someone young and thin enough to wear leggings.

Soooo, as soon as my semester ends, I'm arranging to drive down with my mother if she is well enough. If she's not up to it, I'll go alone. I hate thinking about it, but we have to put the apartment on the market. Every month that my mother continues to own that place is a big drain on her limited resources.

Last night I dreamed that we were waiting in the empty apartment for the guys from Goodwill to come for my father's clothes. When they came, there were four of them and they all looked exactly like my father. I woke up crying.

I wake up crying a lot now, so I'm kind of used to it. But that morning the phone was ringing as I dried my tears on the pillow case. The sight of the empty space next to me was an agonizing reminder of the hole Sol had left in my life. It never failed to bring new tears to my eyes. By the time I collected myself enough to answer the phone, the machine had picked up.

"Bel, Marlene Proletariat here. I hope I catch you before you leave. Sol's been crashing at the studio. There's room, since I live with my fiancé, Joel, at his place in Jersey City now. Anyway I thought you might want to know that Sol's coming over to your house to get his things this afternoon. He thinks you have some kind of meeting and won't be there. I thought you might want to surprise him. He's pretty pissed but also pretty broken up. Good luck."

My apologies to Marlene. Fortunately the woman need never know of the unfeminist curses I'd been heaping upon this paragon of sisterhood in the last few days. Thanks to her alert, I was curled up in the loveseat in the living room, cuddling Virginia Woolf, when I heard Sol's key in the lock. It hadn't take me two seconds to resolve to miss the monthly department meeting and go home right after my morning classes ended. Pearl and Ma had taken a cab to Ma's friend Sofia's house. "Sofia's a great grandmother, Sibyl. *Her* granddaughter Janet has two kids. She's bringing the new baby over to visit Sofia today." I couldn't believe that Ma was actually making me feel guilty because my children were waiting until they could support themselves to have children. Thank God I was too preoccupied to dwell on this.

"Bel." Sol's eyes widened at the sight of me, but otherwise he showed no emotion. "I came to get my things. It's the second Tuesday of the month, so I figured you'd be out this afternoon. It'll just take me a few minutes." He started up the stairs.

I couldn't stand how formal he was. Each clipped phrase nicked my heart. "Sol. I want to talk to you. Please, can't we talk? Let me put on some water." I was following him.

"Thanks, Bel, but I've no time for tea." Was he being sarcastic? We were both in the bedroom now. He pulled a plastic garbage bag out of his pocket and began tossing all the mail from his desk into it. I felt short of breath.

"Well then if you won't have tea and you won't talk, you'll have to listen," I said brattily.

"Yeah. So what else is new?" He *was* being sarcastic. Good. That was better, more real, than that formal tone he'd been using before.

"Sol, I don't want you to leave. I love you. I'm truly sorry about the scene when you came home. You see, Vinny Vallone was killed and they were about to arrest one of my students, so I had to . . ." I was begging and blurting things out all at once. *What's wrong with me?* I thought. *Why can't I be more logical? Why do I sound so pathetic? Where is my famous persuasive ability when I really need it?*

"Bel." Sol had opened a drawer and was picking up stacks of boxers and T-shirts and dumping them into the garbage bag on top of the mail. "You just don't get it, do you? It's not about you and your goddamn students this time. It's about you and me sharing a life." He stopped emptying the drawer and looked at me and then went on, his voice softening a little. "I mean sharing a lifestyle, Bel." Sol was running the fingers of one hand through what was left of his hair, a gesture I recognized with a pang. But then his voice hardened perceptibly again, and he said curtly, "I don't live the way you do."

I took another tack, trying to sidetrack him. "If you're talking about Ma, I can't do anything about that. She needs to be with me right now. She's still a little confused. I'm sorry if you're inconvenienced . . ." Even I heard the edge of anger in my voice at that last line. Sol pounced on it almost before the words had left my lips.

"Inconvenienced? Nice try Bel, but this isn't about Sadie either. I'd do the same for my mother." " He sounded triumphant as he caught me in my pathetic attempt to distract him from the Vinny issue.

"It's about you getting involved with criminals and not even telling me about it." He actually put down the plastic bag. "Why didn't you even tell me about Vinny Vallone's murder? Were you so pissed that I was gone so long that you decided to punish me by not telling me about Vinny? That's it. I'm right, aren't I? You were angry at me for being away so long." He opened a new drawer, picked up the plastic bag again and started tossing in balls of rolled up socks.

"In a way, you're right, I guess." I had sat down on the edge of the bed and was looking the other way. I couldn't stand to see him pack anymore. "But Sol, I really figured this would be over before you got home. I didn't want to upset you." I heard another drawer open.

"I thought I heard you up here, dear," said Ma, coming into the room and planting a kiss on my lower jaw. Neither of us had heard Sadie clump up the stairs behind her walker. "It's Bel and Sol, Pearl," she shouted downstairs. Then she leaned on the rail of the walker, turned to Sol, and said, "Hello Sol. Welcome back. We've missed you."

I almost passed out. This was the most civil greeting my mother had ever extended to Sol. He dropped the new plastic bag he'd just opened and took her hand. "Hello Sadie. I was very sorry to hear about Ike. You know how I felt about him." It was true. Sol and Ike had been close. Sol's voice was thick with empathy and sincerity.

I could see my mother fighting tears. She squared her narrow shoulders and said, "Thank you, Sol. He was quite a guy, and we all miss him. You were a favorite of his." With a teary twinkle in her eye she continued. "Ike used to say that you were Bel's real Mr. Right. . . ." A little sob escaped her, but then out of the corner of her eye, she spotted the plastic bag and the open drawer.

I swear, at that moment the tears crawled back inside Ma's eyes, and I heard Sadie Bickoff say, "And you are moving out now? Gone for most of the year and now, just when she needs you, leaving again? Well Mr. Eastern Europe, it's none of my business, and she'll kill me for saying so, but let me tell you that if you walk out the door, you are a bigger fool than I ever thought you were."

Whatever she was now, my mother was not confused. She spoke with absolute certainty. In fact, she didn't speak. She pronounced. Part of me was cheering her on. Part of me recoiled with shame. "My daughter may be a little meshugah, a little impulsive, and a lot with the mouth, but do you know what the odds are you'll ever find another woman as smart and brave and good as she is? Or one who cares about you like she does? One in a zillion." Sadie paused for breath and then, as an afterthought, went on. "And most of the time, she's beautiful too. Except now she needs a little makeup. She doesn't sleep much. Sibyl, honey, what've you got against Estée Lauder?"

This was Ma talking. The woman always could take the fizz out of a compliment faster than you could say "impossible to please." But even as I chafed, I rejoiced to realize that no one would describe her as disoriented anymore.

And she was still speaking. "Anyway, take it from a woman who was married sixty years to the *same person*." Without missing a beat she gave me a little look. "May he rest in peace, Ike knew you don't settle anything by walking away."

Ma stood poised as if she wanted to say still more, but thinking better of it, turned and made her awkward exit sideways through the door. Sol and I almost tripped over ourselves getting to the stairs to walk in front of her in case she wavered on the way down.

Once downstairs Ma disappeared into her room. Either she needed a nap or she was experiencing a rare moment of tact. Pearl had left when she realized I was home. Sol and I stared awkwardly at each other and then, as if by agreement, headed for the kitchen. I put the kettle on, and this time Sol didn't refuse. Over some jasmine tea we looked at each other across the table.

Ma's outburst had left me uncharacteristically speechless. I was struggling to process the changes in her and digest what she had said all at once. Sol took advantage of my silence by saying softly, "She's really something else, your mom. She's absolutely straight. When she couldn't accept me, she never pretended. Treated me like shit, actually." He shook his head, probably recalling Sadie's many snubs. "Now, for some reason, she's changed her mind and, wow, she's letting me know. I could live with a woman like that, Bel. I used to. What happened to her?" He reached over and stroked my cheek.

I spoke slowly, thinking out loud, really. "I hate it when we fight. But I don't want to give up being who I am and, lately, who I am seems to involve doing a little low-level detective work just like being who you are involves doing a lot of traveling." I tried to inject some spirit into my voice when I spoke next, but I didn't feel very feisty. I felt sad. "I don't want to curtail your freedom. You'd hate that. I don't want you to curtail mine either."

"Telling me you're angry that I'm away so much isn't the same as telling me to stay home. You know that. I'm capable of making my own decisions. Getting involved in the Vinny mess is bad enough. Not telling me about it is cutting me out of your life." Sol's voice had thickened again and he looked away, blinking.

We talked for hours. "Talked" is, perhaps, the wrong word. We cried, laughed, and at times shouted, as I updated Sol on the last few weeks' events. I left out nothing, including what we were planning for that evening. That's when Sol yelled, "What the hell's the matter with you? You can't be serious. Breaking into a car is a crime. You could get arrested, lose your job, maybe even go to jail! And what if he sees you? He's already tried to kill you. If he catches you breaking into his car, he'll try again. Christ, Bel, I thought all this mishegas was over when you started wearing that estrogen patch." Sol had stood up and was pacing around the small kitchen as he ranted.

He must have awakened Sadie, who came in looking rumpled and sleepy. She observed innocently, "Ah. You two are talking things out. That's good."

And we were and it was. Sol was home at last. I

have to admit I had a brief flash of "gotcha" when I finally said, "Thanks for letting me know how you really feel. This thing tonight is something I just have to do. Finding Vinny's killer matters to me. If I didn't try to do it, I wouldn't be me." We both knew what I meant this time.

"God knows, I wouldn't want you to be anyone else, Bel. But just because you have to do it, doesn't mean I have to like it. And I don't." He took my hand across the table and gave it a squeeze. "And I'm not about to pretend I do either."

Sol didn't get a chance to empty those plastic bags of underwear and socks back into his dresser drawers until after I went to work the next day.

Chapter 26

March 27, 1996

Dear Ma Bel,

So how's life in deepest Jersey? It was awesome to talk with you and Grandma last week. You sounded pretty stressed, but Grandma sounded more like her old self.

Just stop worrying. Everything here is fine. Kibbutz activities are winding down with lots of parties and special dinners. It'll be hard to say good-bye. But I still have the trip with Batsheva to look forward to, and then maybe I can get a job here. My Hebrew's pretty good now, and it's much easier to find work over here than it is at home, believe me.

Speaking of Batsheva, she's never been to the states and is thinking of visiting after I go home. I said she could come and stay with us for a while, just a few months until she gets a job. That's cool isn't it? Do you know anything about what's involved in her getting a visa so she could work in the U.S.? (She teaches yoga and meditation.) I said I'd check it out.

So do you have any info? I figure you could ask some of your students. Is it true if you marry an American, you automatically get a visa?

Kiss Grandma Sadie for me. Best to Sol.

Love,
Mark

Which was worse, my baby boy dodging bombs in Israel, or my baby boy marrying the unknown Batsheva and the two of them moving in with Sol, Ma, and me? Fortunately there was no time to dwell on the implications of Mark's latest letter. I had to meet Illuminada and Betty that very night at nine sharp. Before I left, I dropped the two spark plugs Henry had given me and the camera and other stuff Illuminada had provided into my purse. I checked to be sure I had my cell phone.

Betty was waiting outside her house when I pulled up. She got in the car and dialed Illuminada. "Okay, now listen up, girl. Bel and I are en route to Paulus Hook from my house. Where is he?" she barked into the tiny phone. Betty's penchant for giving orders made her a natural for a maneuver like this. So did her desire to stand by her man. If we could get the goods on Arthur, Victor would be home free. I could tell she was eating the whole thing up. I, on the other hand, was counting the minutes until it was over.

"Illuminada says he's parked right on Essex near the corner farthest from the condo. She can't remember the name of the damn street, but it's on the other end of the condo. She says he's walking toward the condo. He hasn't seen her. Oh Lord. She says he's inside now. Okay girl, let's go for it. She's double-parking until she hears from one of us."

Within minutes I had pulled up and found a parking space around the corner from Arthur's blue Toyota. Everything was going according to plan. If Arthur did leave the condo, Illuminada would warn us by cell phone.

We were looking for messages from a corpse: bloodstains, hair, ripped upholstery or other signs of a struggle. Not for nothing had I been force-fed the gory details of the O. J. Simpson trial for months. I had a feeling that, like O. J.'s Bronco, Arthur's car would provide some of the evidence we needed.

Betty got out of my car first and walked to the corner. There she would watch for pedestrians or police. We had no surefire plan for what we'd do if anyone came by, but we were confident that I could find what we sought fast enough to make the risk of discovery negligible. I got out of my car and, pulling on my gloves, walked quickly toward Arthur's blue station wagon.

Stopping about ten feet away, I opened my purse and took out one of the spark plugs Henry had given me. I recalled his instructions. "Throw it like a football." Seeing my brow scrunch up in perplexity at that useless metaphor, he had quickly translated. "Hold it by this here metal end so the smallest white part points at the middle of the window. Then give it a spin toss." Again he patiently translated and demonstrated. "No, throw it like this from back of your shoulder and turn your wrist when you let go. When that sucker hit the window, it break like a egg, only quieter."

Looking back toward the corner, I could see Betty's stocky frame silhouetted in the glow of the streetlight. "Here goes," I coached myself, grabbing the metal end of the spark plug, aiming the point at the window, and heaving and twisting with most of my might. "Bull's-eye! Yes!" It was all I could do to keep from shouting and jumping up and down in triumph when I saw the glass disintegrate and shower the car door and the curb with glitter. I wouldn't even need the extra plug Henry had made me take along in case I screwed up my first effort.

I glanced at Betty, prepared to give her a thumbs-up sign, and froze. Betty stood chatting with a man in sweats whose back was to me. She could see me. What if he turned around? Then I remembered who he was talking to. If Betty didn't want him to turn around, he wouldn't. But I was spooked and shaky when I recovered enough to move.

Quickly I approached the car, unlocked the door, stuck my head in, and looked around the interior, now visible in the light from the ceiling bulb. Illuminada had told me what to do. She would have done it herself, except if she were caught, she could lose her PI license while I, the denial queen, had refused to even consider the possibility of getting caught. I whipped out Illuminada's camera and began photographing everything but disturbing nothing.

There were stains on the headrest of the front passenger seat. I gagged. I couldn't see well enough to find hairs, but I spotted something else. On the floor of the back seat on the driver's side there was a bottle of some chemical with the word CAUTION clearly visible and a few cloths. There were two boxes of kitchen matches. And folded neatly under the bottle, matches, and rags were papers. What looked to me like diagrams filled the part of the papers I could make out. Suddenly flashing back to Arthur's speech on landlord arson, I shuddered. Then I willed my hands to stop trembling and took several pictures of this disturbing collection of artifacts.

After quietly closing the car door, I dialed Illuminada, my gloved fingers clumsy. I sneaked a glance at Betty just in time to see the man she had been talking to wave cheerily at her. I heard him call over his shoulder, "So sorry to have startled you. Good to see you, Betty. Give our best to Randy," as he jogged off in the opposite direction.

Betty told me later that this chatty runner had a son who was an old friend of her son Randy. He just happened to be jogging by and, recognizing Betty, had stopped to say hello. She had told him she was on the way to her car from a friend's house in the area and kept his back to me the whole time I was breaking the car window and getting inside the car. He never saw me. She deserves an Oscar.

Betty and I had just walked the half block to my car when we heard the sirens. It seems Illuminada Guttierez, PI, had reported witnessing a thug break into a car she had been following. She told the cops that the car was full of evidence crucial to the Vallone murder. She also suggested that the fire department might want to send somebody to examine the contents of the car. No, she hadn't seen the perpetrator of the break-in up close. "He was big though," she'd told them. "Built like a football player."

Chapter 27

To: Caregiverssupport@sos.com
From: Bbarrett@circle.com
Subject: Better days, worse nights
Date: 04/07/96 05:15:24

Well, let's hear it for Dr. De Cento again. Not only has he reduced my mother's confusion by taking her off Valium, but he has persuaded her to have a series of shots of some new gel into her knee. He says this should relieve her pain for at least six months and then we can reevaluate.

She no longer gets mixed up about who's dead and who's alive and who's here and who's not. She's back to being the mother I know and love. (Yesterday she suggested I have a total makeover to celebrate Passover.)

She goes to the local senior center, where she has made friends with Sofia Dellafiorno. Now they go to Atlantic City on the bus together. Last week she won a thousand dollars playing those damn machines! She's starting to have a life again, and so am I. I can actually leave her alone in the house, although I don't like to.

The sad part is that now she really feels the loss of my father. Sometimes I wonder if she wasn't better off when she was disoriented and thought he was still with her. I hear her crying at night and see her eyes fill up at odd times. I feel the same way. I hope it will get easier.

"*Dios mio!* The salmon is delicious, Betty. What did you season it with? Is it marinated?" Illuminada can't even pay a compliment without asking a lot of questions.

"I'll give you the recipe," replied Betty, passing the platter of fish to Sol.

"Great veggies too," I chimed in, savoring the garlic-infused spinach.

"I can't take the credit for that. That's one of Vic's mother's recipes," Betty said. "He made it."

Vic said with a twinkle in his eye: "Yeah. I'm the sous chef." Everybody laughed at his playful acknowledgment of Betty's desire to run things. She was actually batting her eyelashes as she passed the salad bowl to Raoul. Things were going well once again.

Although the overt purpose of this gathering was to celebrate solving Vinny's murder, we all knew that the covert purpose was for us to get to know Vic Vallone. Illuminada and I had been after Betty in not-so-subtle ways to bring us all together. Illuminada had asked, "Are you ashamed of us, *chiquita*? I promise not to eat with my hands. And I'll bet he's even forgiven Bel by now."

"Maybe she's afraid one of us will steal him away, I teased. Maybe she's worried that he'll be swept off his feet by a nosy, vertically challenged Latina or a voluptuous and sensual midlife Jewess. . . ."

Betty had finally invited us all to dinner. She'd also invited Pearl Hoskins. Henry had dropped Pearl off along with a pecan pie she had made that would forever redefine dessert for us all. Sol and I had brought some Hoboken bread and several bottles of wine. Illuminada's mother had been invited too, but she had a cold, so she sent her addictive flan. Ma had gone to bed early, since she and Sofia were taking the nine-o'clock bus to Atlantic City the next morning.

"So my grandson's gonna get to finish college now and be a undertaker like he wants. I owe it all to the Good Lord and to you," Pearl said, raising her glass of Sprite high and beaming around the table at all of us.

"Well Pearl, you know I certainly couldn't have done a thing without you. And Henry helped too. Remember, he saved my life," I replied, sipping my wine.

"Here! Here! I'll drink to that." Sol raised his glass high in the air before taking a healthy swig.

"And Henry taught Bel to break car windows! You should have seen her. She was something else!" It was Betty, giggling. She had been giggling a lot lately.

"Here's to all the poor souls in that condo who almost got roasted in their beds," said Illuminada, shaking her head. "*Caramba!* I still can't believe that boy was going to set fire to that building with his own mother in it."

"I visited his mother last week," I said quietly.

"You did what? Why would you visit that nasty old lady?" Illuminada inquired.

"I felt sorry for her, I guess. I brought her some soup," I explained. "I mean, her kid is on trial for murder." I sounded almost apologetic. "She told me that Arthur had started acting sort of odd. 'Dumber than usual' was actually how she put it. He hit her a few times. She got so upset that, without telling him, she wrote him out of her will. She decided to leave her condo, which is all she has, to her church. Arthur overheard her talking to her lawyer about it, and he kind of went off. Broke her jaw. She figures that's when he got the idea about burning down the building. Not only would she die, but he'd get the insurance money."

"I be prayin' for them two." It was Pearl, of course. "Myself, I don't be sittin' in judgment on nobody." Illuminada looked momentarily chastened.

To my surprise, Vic Vallone added, "I've been praying for them too. Ever since Betty told me about Arthur and why he killed my brother . . ." His eyes weren't playful now. In fact, he looked sad. Betty left her seat and stood behind him.

"But I'm glad it wasn't Gilberto," said Victor, still sounding melancholy. "And I'm glad he isn't HIV positive too." He reached behind him for Betty's hand.

"What accounted for your change of heart?" I asked, recalling how angry Victor had been at Gilberto. I had been surprised last week when Gilberto told me that Victor had called him, apologized for hitting him, and offered him a full-time job. I knew that, in turn, Gilberto had apologized for his half-hearted attempt at blackmail.

"After you came to grill me and then Betty broke off with me, I did a lot of thinking. I even talked with Father Santos. I finally realized that Gilberto had made my brother happy and that Vinny had loved him. Since my divorce, I had been so lonely myself that I had envied Vinny, my own brother, his great love."

This somber and forthright assertion had a predictable effect on the evening's festivities. There was total silence. If you ever want to ruin a dinner party, say something sincere, deep, and important. Fortunately,

Betty was too happy to remain silent for long. Raising her glass, she said, "Well, I'm sure glad you didn't kill your brother, but I may just have to kill my son." A burst of laughter greeted Betty's threat just in time to lighten our mood. Everybody within earshot knew that only two days ago Randy had called from Michigan to say he'd totaled his car. Thank God he was uninjured and hadn't hurt anybody, but he was going to have to do a lot of explaining and a lot of work to replace his car and pay for the hike in Betty's auto insurance.

After we had finished the main course, Pearl and Illuminada and I forcibly restrained Betty in the living room while the guys scraped the plates and loaded the dishwasher. "You ever meet a man who can load a dishwasher right?" she fumed. "If they mess up that machine . . . and my fridge is going to be a mess. They'll put everything everywhere. I'll have to spend all morning reorganizing. . . ."

Pearl was too polite to contradict her hostess, but Illuminada minced no words: "*Dios mio*, let it go Betty. Leave them alone. Think of it as male bonding, not dishwashing."

"Yeah," I chimed in. "Men bond when they do things together. So they might as well wash dishes, right?"

"You know," I said when we got Betty settled with a glass of sherry, "this semester I had two students who were really crazy. That's never happened before. I've never had students who were dangerous."

"There's always somebody at risk in a college population. Look at those kids who kill their roommates or their lovers or shoot their teachers because they don't like their grades. And a certain percentage rape their dates and commit suicide." Illuminada was speaking in her matter-of-fact Criminal Justice professor voice. She was right.

I sighed. "Yeah. I know. I just hate to think of my students as contributing to crime statistics, that's all. I'm thinking a lot about this now because I'm planning a paper about the interface between the personal and the pedagogical in the community college classroom for my seminar. But I'm being too serious. Let me spread a little good news."

"Please do. It's a party, after all," said Betty, daintily sipping her sherry.

"Rebecca called me just before Sol and I left the house. She's back at work now. The cast came off last week. But I knew that. That's not why she called."

I paused to take a sip of my sherry, and Illuminada said in an exaggeratedly sweet voice, "Oh don't tell us why she called, Bel. Just keep us guessing. We don't mind."

I ignored her. "Rebecca couldn't wait to tell me that Mark wrote her that he'll be home May fifteenth! He's planning to surprise me." My grin must have left my face and stretched clear across the room.

"Excellent! But why did she tell you? And what happened to the trip with the girlfriend?" Illuminada was, as usual, zeroing in with the right questions.

"Rebecca's incapable of keeping a secret. And she knows how worried I've been, so she wanted me to sleep easier. And I am. There are now only twelve more days until he and his laundry arrive." I raised my sherry glass and we clinked.

"But what about the girlfriend?" Betty insisted.

"Well, she may come later. It seems Mark's college roommate got Mark a summer job waiting tables with him at a posh resort in Maine. He should make decent money and he loves Maine. He can save money there too. I'm just so glad there are no suicide bombers in Maine."

"That means Mark will be home in time to go to Charleston with you and Sol and your mother to empty her apartment," Betty said, wasting no time in organizing my life.

"Amen," said Pearl. "Sadie be happy 'bout that too." Then she stood. "I better get my pie on the table. You gettin' your flan?" She looked at Illuminada.

"Oh let the guys do it," said Betty, stretching luxuriously in her leather easy chair. "And they can make the damn coffee too, while they're at it." Illuminada and I looked at each other and grinned.